To Simon

Best Wishes,

Penelope Keith

CH00951953

To the
Manor Born

To the Manor Born

PETER SPENCE

St. Martin's Press
New York

TO THE MANOR BORN

Copyright © 1979 by Peter Spence
All rights reserved. For information, write:
St. Martin's Press, Inc. 175 Fifth Ave., New York, N.Y. 10010
Manufactured in the United States of America

Library of Congress Cataloging in Publication Data

Spence, Peter.
  To the manor born.

  I. Title.
PZ4.S4728To 1980   [PR6069.P44]   823'.914   79-21559
ISBN 0-312-80752-X

1

If one had been present at the moment Rolls met his Royce, Marks his Spencer, or Gilbert his Sullivan, one might have sensed something historic was in the air. But witnesses to an encounter now about to take place in a remote corner of the English countryside could not have forseen the social upheaval that was to come. Indeed why should they? At that moment, there were no signs and wonders: there were no comets seen, no fingers wrote '*Mene, Mene*' on walls, no pictures fell from them, and the only clock in the vicinity which might have stopped wasn't working anyway.

This was on the spire of the little country church of St Botolphe. The clock face said 8.43 — rust on mould. It should have said 2.25 — gold on blue. It was one of the churches in a parish consisting of a cluster of adjacent villages: Marlbury St Botolphe, Marlbury St Michael, Marlbury St Agnes, and Marlbury St Nicholas, clearly the historic homes of four saints who never really got on. The spartan church, built in the sixteenth century, a time when mortification of the flesh was fashionable and since when no concessions had been made to changing ideas of comfort, was strategically sited on the estate to be within easy reach of the farming community it served — that is to say, to be within sight of at least two other church spires, for the benefit of successive steeplechasing squires. Now, from its west door, there effused the unmelodious wheezing of a bronchial harmonium, every note played usurping the wind already allocated to every other note and giving off a tuneless mush.

The church was filling up and the rector, dressed for action in cassock, surplice and stole, welcomed his sombre congregation with high spirits inappropriate for the occasion, for he had never seen his church so full, let alone on a Tuesday afternoon. When the last of the congregation was settled, he walked down the church path to the lychgate and waited. It was a beautiful autumn afternoon and the estate was looking magnificent. The leaves of the trees and bushes which carpeted and curtained the far side of the valley were just turning, presenting a mosaic effect of golds, coppers, bronzes and crimsons. In the distance, at the top of the far ridge, those trees more exposed to the wind were already bare and stood clearly silhouetted tickling the skyline, arrayed along the horizon like a brush salesman's samples.

So enthralled was the rector by the beauty of the parish in which providence had placed him that he didn't hear a car drive up alongside him. This was not unreasonable since mechanical stealth is one of the boasts of this particular make of car, which could count itself among the fruits of that meeting between Mr Rolls and Mr Royce.

'Excuse me', said a highly polished voice, as a window slid down with a gentle hum which beat for musicality anything that was issuing from the church.

The rector was looking at a very elegant man, with sun-tanned complexion and well-groomed black hair and moustache flecked with grey. He was wearing a yellow turtleneck pullover under a wide-checked sports jacket, which seemed to accentuate the solid squareness of his build and broadness across the shoulder.

This was Richard DeVere — the first party to the imminent meeting.

'Is this the Grantleigh estate?' enquired Richard DeVere.

'Indeed it is,' replied the rector.

6

DeVere consulted a printed sheet which he had taken from his pocket.

'I'm looking for the old lodge,' he said, waving a picture of the said building under the rector's nose.

'You've just passed it. Go back down the road here to the triangle, and you know where Mrs Hodges lives...?'

DeVere sighed. 'If I knew where Mrs Hodges lived, the chances are I would know where the old lodge was.'

'Well, it's next door. First house on the right after the cottage on the left.'

'Thank you.'

'Tell me, who owns this estate?' asked DeVere.

'Mr fforbes-Hamilton.'

'Do you know where I can find him?'

'He'll be here in just a moment.'

'Good. I'd like a word with him.'

'I doubt if you'll get much out of him,' said the rector with an impish look in his eye. 'Ah, here he comes.'

The two men looked down the narrow road, with its high banks winding away through a tunnel of beech trees. A large black limousine turned the corner and entered the tunnel. Its roof adorned with flowers, and it contained a coffin.

'Is that him?' said DeVere.

'Was,' corrected the rector, without a hint of compassion.

'I'm sorry,' said DeVere solemnly.

'No need to be,' chirped the rector. 'We're not.' The rector indicated that perhaps the Rolls-Royce was blocking the approach of the funeral cortège of three cars which was now processing towards them. DeVere, uncharacter-istically unnerved by the approach of the death, even though it wasn't his own, was anxious to oblige, and drove off towards them.

As the cars crept past each other, DeVere could not fail to notice the lady sitting in the back of the second car, clearly

7

the chief mourner, and obviously taking this role very seriously. She wore black and dabbed her eyes with a handkerchief under her veil. This was Audrey fforbes-Hamilton, and this was the meeting which, if the parties had known at the time what was to result from it, would not have passed unnoticed.

'Roadhog,' Audrey muttered as she was driven past.

They both continued on their way to their respective appointments. Richard DeVere to his mission at the old lodge, and Audrey to spend a very pleasant afternoon at her husband's funeral.

There are several good views of Grantleigh Manor nestling as it does in the cusp of the valley. And that may have been the intention of architects who, at the end of the eighteenth century, designed it not with front, back and sides, but with four picturesque, and equally presentable façades. Each elevation was generously pock-marked with windows in the manner of the pre-electric age to make full use of every shaft of daylight available. But perhaps the best vantage point is afforded by the old lodge.

This was only a matter of 200 yards away which meant that, not only could one get a good view of the whole west side and much of the ornamental garden, but one could also see into the rooms like a dolls' house — making it an excellent hide from which to have observed the lifestyle of the landed gentry for nearly two centuries. It was from this viewpoint, from the terrace of the old lodge, that Richard DeVere now caught his first traumatic glimpse.

'Now, that's what I call a house,' he marvelled.

The way he said it left one in no doubt that the building from which he was viewing it was not what he would call a house. Pity, since it was for sale.

This opinion stirred considerable anguish in the heart of one Julian Anderson, who was standing behind him in the empty drawing room of the old lodge. He was the estate agent whose company, Anderson & ffitch, were trying to off-load the old lodge on to some monied person, prepared to pay over the odds for this 'tasteful period conversion in private secluded valley'. In thinking that DeVere could be coaxed and cajoled into buying it by sales talk and blandishments on the strength of this one viewing, he underestimated him. He knew little about him, except that his general demeanour and transport suggested he was not short of the negotiable tender, and that he was looking for a house in the west country for his ageing mother and her 'staff'. As DeVere continued to gaze transfixed at the manor, Anderson knew that from that moment consideration of the old lodge had been abandoned like a child's Christmas present on the arrival of a bigger parcel with brighter wrapping.

'Will you be handling that when it comes up for sale?' asked DeVere.

'The manor? For sale? No chance.'

'But the old man's dead, isn't he?'

'If you mean Marton fforbes-Hamilton, yes. But he was hardly an old man. Dead at forty-six.'

'Tragic.'

'Not really, but we would so much rather it had been her.'

This was the second time the character of the deceased had been impugned, and now his widow was being implicated as well.

'Tell me more,' he said, 'about *her*.'

'Audrey?'

'Yes.'

'She was a cousin of Marton's. The family has been here for centuries. Came over with William the Conqueror and never got out of the habit of throwing their weight about.'

'Is there an heir now?' DeVere asked.

'No children at all.'

9

'So the line ends there?'

'I suppose it does.'

'So put two and two together.'

DeVere had already done so in his very incisive mind. He had seen from the state of the place, its rough edges and need of paint and masonry work, that the owner did not have money to throw around. It followed that the place was probably hocked for working capital in a tight agricultural and economic climate. The owner had probably raised everything he could on the strength of his trump card — a life expectancy which would perhaps take him through to easier times. Then he'd done the worst thing a landowner could do. He'd died in possession, thereby exposing himself to crippling sanctions — death duties and the like. Anderson was put out by his client's familiarity with his own field.

'Besides, one little widow is going to rattle in a place that size. I bet it will be on the market within a month.'

'You could be right.'

'You bet I am. Let's go and have a look at the place.'

Anderson wavered.

'I don't think we should. If you'll excuse my saying so. Besides, Mrs fforbes-Hamilton isn't in.'

'I know — she's at the old man's funeral. She'll be tied up for a while.'

'Isn't that taking an unfair advantage?'

'This is business, Mr Anderson. There's no sentiment in business. Am I wrong?'

'Only in one respect. She's hardly a little old widow.'

'I look forward to meeting her.'

The two men set off from the terrace, across the lawn and through the gate into the manor garden.

That intriguing little statistic which holds that there are more people alive today than have ever lived and died in the whole history of mankind, seemed to be born out by the scene in the little churchyard on the Grantleigh estate. For every fforbes-Hamilton in it, or under it, and the churchyard was full of them, there appeared to be two or three live ones now processing out of the church, to see their latest casualty change sides. Added to the family were a host of good friends and neighbours, the entire estate work-force, and assorted busy-bodies and rubber-necks, so it seemed that Marton's funeral was a very popular event.

He was now going to join his ancestors, who availing themselves of their exclusive burial rights in this particular little corner of England, were now at rest. Their epitaphs, like 'Tally Ho' and 'Gone to ground', evoked the huntsmen's 'Peel's view Hulloo' for which the old song claims power to waken the dead, but which in this respect was today failing miserably.

The mourners gathered solemnly round the grave with family to the fore. They all looked bored enough to have actually been listening to the rector who was intoning random texts.

'He walked in the way of the Lord, and served him right,' he chanted.

He motioned the undertakers to lower the coffin as he continued the order of service.

'For as much as it hath pleased Almighty God — to take unto himself our dear brother Marton here departed, we therefore commit his body to the ground.'

'Would you like to throw the sod in, Mrs fforbes-Hamilton?' whispered the rector.

Audrey's first thought was that this was no way to talk about her husband, but the rector, handing her a little trowel full of earth, salvaged it.

'Earth to earth, ashes to ashes, dust to dust, in sure and certain hope of the resurrection to eternal life. Aimen.'

'Armen,' said Audrey, part responding, part correcting, and handing back the empty trowel.

11

The rector snapped the Bible shut and stood for a few moments with his head bowed. Then he took Audrey by the arm, and drew her away from the graveside.

'Well, there we are, Mrs fforbes-Hamilton, and may I say if I can help you at all at this time of mourning, I shall only be too happy. The clergy have a great contribution to make to people's sorrow.'

'Thank you, rector,' said Audrey, politely. 'It was a lovely funeral. We must have another one sometime. I do hope you can join us for a drink at the manor.'

The mention of a drink warmed the cockles of his little clerical heart.

'Thank you,' he said. 'Do you realize that this is the tenth fforbes-Hamilton I've buried in this churchyard? So it does call for a little celebration. If you get my meaning.'

Audrey didn't.

'May I see you to your car?' the rector offered, propelling her towards an old black Rolls-Royce.

'No, I'll walk back to the manor through the garden, thank you.'

She turned away and yelled, 'Brabinger.'

A rotund, bespectacled family retainer in a bowler hat who was tottering towards the car with a little beagle on the end of a lead, stopped and turned round. He was the butler.

'Could you give me that instruction again, please, madam?' he begged, pointing to his hearing aid.

'I haven't given it to you the first time yet,' said his mistress, with evident irritation. 'Just let Bertie off the lead for a bit of exercise, would you? He can come with us. Marjory!'

Marjory Frobisher, a spidery figure with staring eyes and a nun-like complexion, in a coat and skirt which looked as if it needed both a wash and a shave, snapped out of her daydream and stepped forward.

'Yes, Audrey, dear?'

'You come with me. We're walking.'

12

'Yes, dear.'

'Come along, Bertie.' Brabinger had let the beagle off the lead. The hound ran straight to a grave, began to burrow, and emerged with a bone.

Audrey screamed at it. 'Bertie, put that bone down. You don't know who it's been!'

Audrey's was the only voice which was being raised above a low murmur.

As chief mourner, that was her privilege. Everybody else was shuffling about, saving anything they had to say until they were at least indoors and warm enough to say it.

'See you all back at the manor,' said Audrey to everyone.

She and Marjory slipped through the kissing gate and soon they were on the path across the paddock, heading for the rose garden at the back of the manor.

Meanwhile at the manor, DeVere was snooping. There could be no pleasanter word for it.

He liked what he saw. It was no surprise to either DeVere or Anderson to find that Grantleigh, house and contents, was a mish-mash of every style and period, and yet its features seemed to fit with all the others, combining comfort with elegance. The garden had its Greek statues rubbing shoulders with Roman caryatids, Egyptian obelisks, darkened and worn by the spray from Italian fountains. Inside the house, Baroque, Romanesque, Rococo, Jacobean — you name it — made companionable room-mates.

The two men were so carried away by this kaleidoscope of antiquity that they ceased to be aware of their own presence, let alone anybody else's. This trance-like state obtained until, having followed a line of portraits of bewhiskered ancestors, and women in frilly bath-hats, all along the upper gallery overlooking the great hall, they found themselves at the bottom of the grand staircase,

13

leaning and panting against two vast pillars of veined marble. Here a broadbeamed matron in an apron bore through the green baize door with the brass tacks which divides master and servants' quarters, skipped past bearing a tray of sausages on sticks and brought them back to the present.

'Afternoon, Mr Anderson,' she said. 'Nice one for it.' She disappeared into the drawing room and they followed.

Audrey and Marjory sauntered across the paddock and were entering the rose garden before either of them spoke. Marjory, a perennial talker, was uncharacteristically silent, and, feeling that it was Audrey's day, was anxious to do nothing to spoil it.

'Well, thank God that's over,' said Audrey.

'It must have been hard for you. You kept your composure very well. You're very brave.'

Audrey ignored the compliment.

'Are we out of sight?'

'I think so;'

'Good. I can take this damned hat off. If there's one thing guaranteed to make a widow feel grisly, it's having to face the immediate future through a veil. It makes me feel like a doomed butterfly in a raspberry patch.'

Audrey stopped. It was her day, so Marjory stopped too.

'Marjory, how long have we been friends?'

'All our lives, just about.'

'And you agree that a great bond of respect and trust has grown up between us...that's if we overlook that little matter of the crush we both had on Cynthia Mores-Fitzsimmons at school.'

'Of course, dear,' said Marjory, wishing Audrey wasn't always having to bring this up.

'Because I don't want you breathe a word of what I'm going to do now.'

14

'Naturally. You have my word. No probs.'

'No probLEMS — I do wish you'd get out of that habit. Now.'

'Nobody is looking are they?' She looked all about her to satisfy herself that the coast was clear.

'Right, here goes.' With that, Audrey underwent a sudden transformation and dissolved into peals of eldritch laughter which echoed through the valley. The convulsion subsided as quickly as it had begun.

'There. I feel so much better now,' said Audrey when she was herself again. Marjory went pale and was still quivering from shock.

'But Audrey, I don't understand.'

'I am a woman, Marjory — a mere woman — a widow of barely a week. I have lost my husband, so you must forgive my little display of emotion. I can't help it.'

'Yes, but...'

'I'm sorry if I embarrassed you, but you can't expect me to go round po-faced like a Japanese Noh-mask all the time. I can't pretend that Marton pegging out like that wasn't the most wonderful thing that ever happened. Just think. The Grantleigh estate all mine now. All I ever wanted. It's too good to be true.'

Marjory was dumbstruck.

'Oh, have I shocked you?' said Audrey, sounding surprised.

'I must say,' faltered Marjory, 'I'm a little taken aback. I know that you and Marton didn't always get on.'

'Well, we do now,' Audrey snapped back. 'Yes, I think I'll adjust to being on my own very nicely. Oh, of course, I'll miss the little things — like having somebody to do up the back of my dress.' She sighed. 'But I suppose I can learn how to slip the zip flap in the top of the wardrobe door and jump off a chair.'

They were getting near the house.

'Now, you won't breathe a word, Marjory, will you?'

'No.'
'Sure?'
'Absolutely pos.'

The drawing room at the manor was laid out for a feast. The white-clothed table whimpered under the weight of fancy foods, cheese and pineapple on sticks, canapés, olives in bacon, vol au vents, cheese dips: the kind of food one doesn't have to open one's mouth for. The party did not look at all promising until DeVere came to the end of the longest table where several ranks of champagne bottles were awaiting consumption. The spread put DeVere in a mild party mood, sufficient to make him light a cigar.

Behind the tables stood ranks of white-coated men and women in black with frilly aprons, with nothing to do but wait. They stared at the two men for want of something better to do, and Anderson felt called upon to speak.

'We won't be long,' he said. The catering manager, Mr Widrig, was looking at his watch in considerable irritation. Everything was ready to serve and there was no-one to serve it to. The champagne was cold and the chipolatas were hot, and unless the guests arrived this minute, the position would reverse. A champagne cork shot across the room propelled by an explosion. DeVere spun round.

'Don't pop the corks,' he shrieked. 'Champagne corks should never be popped. They should be eased off.'

'I'm sorry,' said a minion, 'but I hear them coming.'

True, everybody could hear the sound of footfalls on the blue-lias floor of the hall.

'I think we'd better go now, Mr DeVere,' said Anderson trying to be casual.

The door opened behind them, and two elderly ruby-jowled men with loud voices and moustaches strode purposefully in, followed by their wives.

16

'Oh, dear, are we the first in?' one of the women was asking in a voice you could scour pans with. 'It must look too awful.' She accepted a drink of champagne.

'Of course, I am longing to ask about the shoot, but this isn't the time,' said one of the old duffers.

'Dashed good shoot, this. Barrels get ruddy hot,' bellowed the other, his voice bouncing off the ceiling and setting a chandelier tinkling. Their wives, whose bodies dammed the doorway, now moved deeper into the room to make way for a sudden rush of people.

'Good afternoon. Lovely funeral,' said one of the women as she brushed past DeVere. DeVere was looking for his best means of escape, but the route through into the hall and front door was becoming a crowded one-way system.

'The french window,' he said, and he and Anderson moved off.

DeVere was one of those people who could not make himself scarce nor be ignored. He had a habit of turning a social gaffe into a grace. People fell away before him, and a waiter put down his tray of drinks to open the french windows for him. They walked on to the terrace, but something made them freeze in their tracks. It was a peal of eldritch laughter wafting across the lawn from the rose garden. Anderson went white, and melted into the drawing room. DeVere stayed his ground.

He caught sight of two women and a creature of some kind — probably a dog — coming towards the manor across the lawn. DeVere slipped behind a pillar and waited, patiently drawing on his cigar.

From behind the pillar, DeVere had a chance to scrutinize the fabled Audrey. She was tall, with a slim figure, and had a proud bearing though rather an odd gait for a woman — long strides — and she dug her feet into the ground, a mannerism born of years of sensible shoes. She did not appear to be the overpowering dreadnought rumour led one to expect. She wore black, a completely styleless

17

coat and skirt, and she was carrying her veiled hat. DeVere allowed that she was not looking her best. Black was clearly not her preference of colour her face suggesting pastel shades; though it certainly seemed to go with that sinister laughter which had echoed from the orchard.

'The ballroom, I thought,' she was confiding. 'I thought that having the funeral party in the morning room smacked too much of a macabre joke. This is no time for gallows humour.'

A puff of cigar smoke came from behind the pillar, which set Audrey's nose twitching.

'Ah — Marianao cigars — memories, memories.'

She traced the effusion to its source. DeVere made no effort to confirm his presence or deny it.

'Correct,' he said at last.

'Then you must be my husband's tobacco merchant.'

She shook his hand.

'No.'

'Then who are you?'

'I'm Richard DeVere. Cavendish Foods.'

'Well, never mind,' said Audrey. 'How very good of you to come.'

'This may not be a good time,' DeVere faltered.

'...it was a great shock. Life must go on,' interrupted Audrey, drawing on her repertoire of funeral pleasantries. 'Won't you come in and have a drink?'

Put like that, how could he refuse? He'd driven the 150 miles from London, and a glass of champagne, and even a cheese dip on a crisp, was better than nothing.

'Thank you,' he said, and followed her back into the drawing room.

The room was crowded by now and the guests were forming groups, polarizing into friends of deceased and employees of same. DeVere spent a very pleasant time in conversation with a very attractive, busty young woman, who turned out to be Lady Mortlake. That he didn't know her identity, marked him down as a stranger to the locality, and he was at once regaled with a potted history of the neighbourhood. From the great volume of information she offered he distilled that she lived on a nearby estate in a stately home by the name of Harborough Hall. In the seventeenth century, her husband's ancestors had been locked in a deadly earnest status rivalry with the fforbes-Hamilton family, each building their extravagant mansions as a display of territorial dominance, and continuing to build wings and annexes at each other and filling them with treasures in a then-prevalent ritual of social sabre-rattling.

The fforbes-Hamilton family insisted that they would have won this war of prestige, were it not for a *fin de siécle* fire, in which the house and contents were destroyed, obliging them to start all over again with the building of the present manor house. She was at pains to explain that although there was speculation that the fire was no accident and that the Mortlakes had a hand in it, the rivalry had long since abated, and she and Audrey were good friends.

'But don't tell her I told you,' she concluded.

DeVere was grateful to have found such a talkative companion, because it meant he didn't have to say much, thereby saving him having to explain his presence.

Although Audrey was circulating grandly, their paths did not cross again to speak to, though they exchanged looks. She appeared to be being bothered by a fat man in a pinstripe suit.

Her flow of 'one must bear it with fortitude' and 'into every life a little rain must fall' was being interrupted by the clawing man.

'Audrey, there are some things I must talk to you about. As soon as possible. In fact, this afternoon as soon as you have a moment. Business, I'm afraid.'

Audrey stopped in her tracks and turned on him.

'Arnold, this is a funeral. You must learn not to combine business with pleasure.'

'It's very important,' the man continued.

'Well, not now. Have you got a drink?'

'Yes, I have,' he said, raising his champagne glass. Audrey seized it.

'Thank you. Now do go and get yourself one.' The man did what he was told.

Marjory was still clinging to Audrey like the bridesmaid she had been twenty years before, and took the opportunity between conversations to question her choice of liquor.

'Champagne, Audrey?' she said. 'I wouldn't have thought that was suitable for a wake.'

'Why not?' Audrey parried. 'And I do wish you wouldn't keep calling it a wake. It makes me think Marton is going to come round and start demanding early morning tea.'

'Well, even tea would be a bit more appropriate.'

'No, the champagne was a good idea,' Audrey insisted. 'I want to use the opportunity to butter up the staff and put their minds at rest about the future of the estate. It'll save having to call them all in later. I do hate having the farm people traipsing through the house, reeking of silage, and treading hayseed into the Wilton. You can always tell when they've been. They help themselves to the After Eights and leave the wrappers. It's very embarrassing when I find myself offering a box of waste paper to the Lord Lieutenant of the county.'

Her tirade tailed off as she looked across the room at DeVere.

'Marjory, who *is* that man over there?'

'Which one?'

'The one dressed like a chessboard. My goodness, some people. Hiring funeral clothes from Moss Bros is one thing, but hiring them from Billy Smart's is unforgivable. Still, he is rather attractive, isn't he?'

Marjory had noticed something of the sort, and was a little shocked to see that Audrey was aware of such things — her husband barely in the grave.

'Well,' said Audrey, anticipating a rebuke and dodging it by changing the subject. 'It's time I said my piece.' She raised her voice. 'Could I have your attention, please, everybody?'

Silence prevailed.

'Thank you,' she began. 'Now, I know that with champagne and with me making a speech, this is rapidly becoming like a wedding.'

There was uneasy laughter. It was her privilege to make jokes, but nobody was sure if it was anybody's privilege to laugh at them.

'Of course,' she went on, 'I'd be the last to suggest that this was anything but a very sad occasion, and I myself am utterly bereft. But life must go on, and I see this not as the end of an era, but the beginning of a new one. I shall continue to run the estate single-handed, and it will march forward with me at the helm.' Her flow was interrupted by a log falling out of the fire. 'I hope I shall be forgiven, but I know that this would be the wish of my dear, dead…loss. I ask you to charge your glasses and drink a toast to what would mean more to him than anything else. The future of the Grantleigh Manor estate.'

Everybody joined in. 'Grantleigh Manor estate.'

'Thank you. Now do enjoy yourselves,' Audrey urged the assembly, as she stepped down from the fender.

'Oh, Audrey,' exulted Marjory as the hubbub around her swelled again. 'What a magnificent speech.'

'Fine words, find words,' added the fat man in the pinstripes — Arnold, the family solicitor. 'But I must talk to you now.'

'Oh, do pipe down, Arnold, can't you leave me to my grief?' Audrey protested dramatically, and walked into the sea of people, who fell back to allow her to pass.

Richard DeVere did not fall back — that was not his style. Besides, he was deep in thought. Audrey's speech had awakened feelings in him. His wife had died six months

21

before. Although stricken to the quick by her death, he too had taken the bit between the teeth and had resolved that life must go on. That was before the facts had sunk in, and time had distanced him from the event sufficiently to see that life could not be the same. Now he knew that changes and adjustment had to be made, at least that the old life had to be allowed to slip away in all but memory. It seemed to him that Audrey was about to make the same mistake, and he sympathized. Now Audrey was standing before him, and he awoke from his reverie.

'I thought you made a magnificent speech, Mrs fforbes-Hamilton. I mean that because I know what you're going through. You see, it was only six months ago that my own wife passed away.'

'Oh, how gratifying,' said Audrey pleasantly. 'I mean, to know that you liked my speech. You're Mr DeVere, aren't you? You must be one of the Berkshire DeVeres. You were once very kind to my husband, I think?'

'Not me. I never knew him.'

DeVere was coming clean. 'No, I've been looking at the old lodge. I want to buy it for my mother, and I seem to have got embroiled in your party.'

'Oh,' said Audrey, drawing herself up to her full height and staring at him loftily. She was disarmed at such a candid admission of gate-crashing.

'Your husband,' DeVere went on. 'I gather from Lady Mortlake that it was pneumonia.'

The mention of Lady Mortlake stirred the competitive spirit.

'Double pneumonia. We fforbes-Hamiltons do nothing by halves.' With that, she sailed into the mêlée and was gone, buttonholing the fat Arnold as she went.

'I thought it was only Americans who were preoccupied with what people die of,' she was muttering. 'Arnold, did you bring that man in?' she asked when they were in a corner by a table littered with cards. 'Is the social scene so

22

depressed that people are reduced to gate-crashing funerals?'

'I don't know,' he confessed. 'I thought he was something to do with you.'

'No. People who have anything to do with me don't have wives who "pass away".' She looked at the array of cards and selected one at random. 'Any more than they go to a happy hunting ground where honeysuckle ever twines, or to a bourne whence no man ever returns. Everybody I know — dies.'

'Not immediately, I'm sure,' comforted Arnold.

'I mean the word. They die, and once they have died, they are dead — I can't do with pretty euphemisms. Now, I think I'll just go and powder my nose.'

'But I must talk to you,' insisted Arnold. 'I know it's not the right time, but when I tell you what it is, you'll understand.'

'Oh, very well. Come on to the terrace.'

They fought their way back into the throng and blazed a trail through the jungle of cocktail conversation before they found a clearing from which they could break loose on to the terrace.

'....play golf? Good God, I'd rather read a book,' were the last words they heard.

'Now what is it? And it had better be very good,' Audrey demanded, after their ears had adjusted to the comparative silence of the terrace.

'It's bad,' burbled the solicitor.

'Then it had better be very bad.'

'It's worse.'

'Then what is it? You're looking about as cheerful as a lovesick bloodhound.'

'Judging from that speech you made, you have no idea what I'm going to tell you.'

'None whatever.'

'How long has my firm represented your family?' This

23

preamble to a subject was familiar to Audrey. Hadn't she used it herself minutes before?

'Oh, you're not going to roar with laughter, are you?'

'Certainly not,' said Arnold.

'Well, what is this all about?'

'You had no idea that Marton was bankrupt? He didn't tell you?'

'He tried not to bother me with little details.'

'Little details!' Arnold carped. 'Don't you realize what this means? It means there's no money — it means that Marton never, strictly speaking, owned the estate.'

'What do you mean?'

'For the last five years it's been mortgaged as collateral against debts — on Marton's death, ownership automatically passes to the bank. The mortgage has been called in.'

'Oh, don't blind me with science, Arnold. What are you telling me?'

'I'm telling you you don't have any alternative.'

'To what.'

'To selling up.'

'Sell up Grantleigh? You're mad.'

'I'm serious, Audrey, I'm sorry.'

'Are you telling me that Grantleigh and the fforbes-Hamiltons have got to part company?'

'Exactly. The creditors are insisting on it. And then there are the death duties.'

Audrey went white and for a moment looked as though she were going to faint. She stared at him in disbelief.

'Have they no sense of history? We've been here through wars, plagues, floods, civil strife, rebellions, famine and Labour governments. We can't let a little thing like a bankruptcy alter the natural course of events.'

'Times change,' Arnold ventured.

'They certainly do not,' Audrey snapped back. She thought for a moment. 'So what are we going to do ?'

'Sell up,' said Arnold matter-of-factly. 'We tried to guide

Marton's affairs, but you know how hopeless he was with money.'

'The fool. If only he'd listened to me.'

'He did.'

'Is there nothing we can do?' said Audrey, adopting an uncharacteristically pleading tone of voice.

'Short of raising the money to buy the place back on the open market — no.'

'Then that's what we must do.'

'Be reasonable, Audrey. Where are you going to find a million pounds?'

'Is that what it costs? Where's my handbag,' she said moving off towards the french window.

'Oh, don't be facetious.'

'I shall if I want to be,' insisted Audrey imperiously. 'A fforbes-Hamilton does not lose his sense of humour in a crisis. Remember Great Uncle Gussy at Malplaquet? The whole thing is unthinkable.' Her voice was choking as a lump came to her throat, and her lip trembled. 'Losing one's husband is one thing — that one can take. But to lose the manor and the estate.' She began to sob; real tears appeared in her eyes and her hitherto dry handkerchief began to moisten. She waved her hands in the general direction of the estate with an expansive gesture.

'Look out there, Arnold. Well, who built all that up to what it is today? Not Marton, no. No, it was me. Me. I did it with my own fair hands and the sweat of my brow.' She paused. 'At least, it was me who sent the men out. And now, it seems, all for nothing.'

She allowed herself one more uninhibited sob and recovered her composure.

'I'm sorry you have to see me like this. I'm not normally given to crying, but since we've joined the Common Market, I seem to have picked up these ghastly continental habits.'

Arnold felt inadequate in the task of consoling her. She

had evidently decided to be disconsolate. Yet he tried.

'Come, come, Audrey — your prospects aren't that bad. There may be a bit left, and you could move out and live quietly somewhere — you'll survive.'

'Away from the manor, I don't see any point in surviving. Really, Arnold, can you honestly see me eking out the rest of my days listening to "The Archers" and waiting for the mobile library?'

'No, I can't. But I can see you pulling through, starting a new life, and remarrying even. You could start getting about and having a good time.'

'But we have work to do.'

'Work?'

'Certainly — you know I'll do anything to stay at the manor. If raising a measly million is what must be done to keep the estate in the family, then that's what we must do. The family has a duty to rally round.' She looked about her as if looking for an orchestra to play some Elgar. 'Not just me, but everybody who goes by our name has a duty to chip in. We'll do it. We'll raise enough between us to pay off these predators...'

'Creditors,' corrected Arnold.

'...and buy Grantleigh back from the bank. Blood is thicker than water.'

'The banks will want something more tangible than water.'

'Blood, then,' announced Audrey flaring her nostrils as the old family bloodlust rose within her. 'Yes, we'll defend the place to the last drop of family blood. We'll fight to the last man.'

Arnold knew that the reaction to his bombshell could go either way. And it had.

'I can't see it,' he said, shaking his head. 'Still, if that's your attitude, I suppose you won't be convinced that you're on to a lost cause until the walls of Grantleigh really are splattered red with the family blood.'

Audrey stiffened.

'Blue, Arnold, blue,' she corrected.

As they returned to the party, they did not notice Richard DeVere lurking behind a pillar.

2

'Would you call this a bay window or a bow window?' said a voice from behind the sofa.

'It's an oriel, silly boy,' snapped Audrey.

The first voice belonged to apprentice estate agent, Murdoch Morrison, a protegé of Julian Anderson. Already, the wheels for the sale of Grantleigh were beginning to turn. The first sign was the arrival of Morrison with a tape-measure and a photographer, who were now wandering about the house taking details and assembling a complete dossier on the property.

'Why can't your people send somebody who doesn't have to keep asking silly questions?' Audrey continued. 'This house deserves at least the attention of an expert and not a callow youth who doesn't know an oriel from a bay window.'

Audrey was in black spirits. She was still in a state of shock. The impact of what Arnold had told her was only just beginning to make itself felt.

Until now, the notion of Grantleigh going up for sale was just a theory, but with the traipsings of surveyor and estate agents, and photographers not by her invitation but on the instructions of Grubb's Bank it had suddenly become a fact. Soon Lady Mortlake would have to know.

She was understandably irritable and in the last few days had withdrawn into herself. She had a lot to think about. But rather than dwell on the question 'how on earth did this

28

happen without my knowing?' she tried to concentrate on the future. It was as well that at this stage she did not for a moment entertain the idea that she would not be able to buy the manor back, or contemplate the seizure of the horses or any change of her social life which would surely have been too much. This was a temporary set-back. She took it for granted that the rest of the family would rally round, but she accepted that for the required amount of money, it would take great effort on her part. It would mean setting up a family trust, and at all costs Grantleigh must stay in the family. It was such a pity that she didn't have time to collar them all at the funeral.

But this was no time for brooding on what might have been; there was work to do. First there were the family archives to research.

Audrey sighed. 'Well, this won't get the baby bathed,' and went into the great hall to order the boxes of family papers up from the cellar. Standing at the bottom of the stairs, dwarfed by the marble pillars, and awed by the excessive dimensions of the stairway and galleries, and that cavernous space in which successive generations had been known to fly kites in the winter draughts, stood young Morrison.

'Is this what you'd call the lobby?' he asked, nervously.

Meanwhile, 150 miles away in the penthouse office of Cavendish Foods, Millbank, London, Richard DeVere was thinking.

He was dissatisfied, and could not account for it. After all, he had little enough to feel unhappy about — a millionaire at forty-six, founding father and head of a massive supermarket chain and food conglomerate, and he had around him all the trappings of wealth and the symbols of success. It should have brought some kind of satisfaction, but suddenly his whole existence had turned

29

sour on him. Maybe all his tycoonery had just been a display of virility and muscle-flexing for the benefit of his wife. Now that she had gone, it had lost its purpose. Now she was dead, he blamed himself for not having spent more time with her, while he pursued what he now considered empty dreams. This regret manifested itself in a sudden surge of concern for the welfare of his little old mother, which by way of atonement, had led him down to the country in search of a retreat for her.

But what was unnerving him was the deep impression that that first sight of Grantleigh Manor had made on him. It was love at first sight, and the idea of owning it and living in it had appealed to him to such an extent, that in the last few days he had thought of little else.

In fact, he resented its intrusion into his life at this stage and all that this sudden burst of admiration was telling him about himself. Its message was that inside this dynamic, jet-setting, hard-living, tough, smart, self-disciplined, go-getter there was an easy-going, idle, shabby, English country gentleman trying to get out. In other words, Grantleigh had demolished his own self-image, but at least it had had the courtesy to replace it with a new one. The conviction that changes had to be made came upon Richard DeVere with some urgency. Even if he couldn't turn his back on one life to embrace a new, he could think of no obstacle to some form of compromise.

'Hilda,' he said into the office intercom.

'Yes, Mr DeVere,' cracked the speaker.

'Get me Anderson and ffitch. You know, that estate agents down in the country.'

Once the 'For Sale' posters were up, the future of the estate became the abiding topic of discussion among the Midianites.

'The Midianites' was Audrey's pet name for all the

families who lived on the estate. She had once observed that if you live in the big house which is the focal point of a community, you are never alone in it, for the estate people are forever in and out. This much they had in common with the biblical Midianites who according to the hymn 'prowl and prowl around' and the name stuck. At first, they couldn't believe it. Some, notably old Ned Peaslake, the farm factotum, who was among the idlest and had been there on sufferance for the last few decades, was delighted to think that the family hold on the valley was to be broken.

Ned was a widower who lived in a tied cottage at Mellow End Mill with his son. The son was the village policeman, an occupation which had assured him of a quiet life these last twenty years, the residents of Grantleigh being a fairly law-abiding lot, give or take the odd poacher. However, Peaslake lived in hope of some momentous crime being committed on his patch, which he would detect, and thereby make his mark in forensic history. In this event, one thing seemed certain, and that was the villain of the piece he envisaged would be Brabinger. There was more to this than the fact that butlers always did it — whatever it was. Peaslake hated Brabinger, as much as did his father Ned, who had hardly exchanged a word with Brabinger for thirty years.

They each had their own vendettas — or perhaps it was the same one. Ned's hostility he could understand since an incident long ago, but Peaslake's grudge was a mystery to Brabinger.

'I'll have you one of these days,' he kept telling him on every meeting. 'Remember '47.'

This puzzled Brabinger, since he could not remember 1947. But whatever happened in '47, it led to a campaign of victimization against Brabinger in his role as chauffeur.

Peaslake had got him for speeding in the Rolls twice, and two endorsements resulted. Brabinger then had a collision with a cow, from which a court case followed, at which

31

Peaslake, as prosecuting constable, felt secure that Brabinger would be hounded from the Queen's highway. Yet, he was acquitted, which caused Peaslake, thinking this was due to Audrey's influence on the local bench, to step up his vendetta which developed against the upper classes in general, and Rolls-Royces in particular.

So many brushes between the two had since taken place on the road, and with Brabinger under a cloud, he had been forbidden by Audrey to drive on the public highway. His chauffering was, therefore, confined to roads on private estates, and as this was where one tended to arrive and depart from great houses, this was the only place the appearance of a chauffeur was needed. Much as Ned and the constable were cheered by the prospect of escape from the thraldom of the fforbes-Hamiltons, they would miss the sport of pursuing their vendetta.

Others had mixed feelings and though they agreed the old regime had been hard but fair, dreaded change purely on the devil-you-know principle. In fact, it was this school of thought which gained momentum from the moment the advertisements for Grantleigh appeared in the national press, and potential buyers started flocking to view the property.

From what the Midianites could see of these interested parties, they could judge that they were all rich. That went without saying, since the current market value of Grantleigh was probably around the million mark. But it was not the kind of richness they were used to. It was the sort of wealth which arrived and departed in helicopters and Commanche and Cherokee private planes, and was represented by swarthy men in flowing robes, little yellow men with short sight and indelible smiles, or big, rowdy men in stetson hats and bootlace ties.

The trickle of buyers for the manor swelled to a torrent, many of whom brazenly announced horrendous plans for the estate.

They were mostly Arabs, Japanese, American and Dutch, and such English as there were spoke with accents which Audrey deemed to be beyond the pale. 'Beyond the Trent' would be nearer the mark, as Audrey regarded anywhere north of the Bristol Channel as tundra.

One of the people who inspected the house turned out to be German and wanted to pull the manor down and just use the land as extra acreage for cabbage, to fill what he called a 'weeping need' for locally produced sauerkraut. Another actually admitted to being a Communist and wanted it as a conference centre for the National Union of Ductile-iron-piping Operatives. There was a pop star whose presence viewing the house set all the local schoolgirls cooing in the surrounding bushes while others handed their autograph books in to Brabinger, who signed them, and handed them back. The pop star wanted to make the house a recording studio and rehearsal centre.

Several government administrators came to consider Grantleigh as a sanatorium. Gurus of alternative living assessed its potential for experiments in psychodrama, and the odd scientist came to see whether it was a suitable place to manufacture germs and viruses.

Throughout, Audrey behaved heroically, welcoming them all as if they were long-lost friends, and never at a loss to explain why Grantleigh was totally inappropriate for their various designs, or to point out structural defects which she invented resourcefully. Her favourite ploy was to have Bertie barking at any convenient empty chair.

'Oh, he's only seen Sir Bedivere,' she would say, pointing to the empty chair. Then she'd tell her ghost story with a gory account of how Sir Bedivere met his death and his more eerie manifestations.

'Been sitting there since Tudor times. Quite mad — he used to wear a codpiece on his nose!' she added for authenticity. That and the story of the headless cyclist worked wonders.

33

Yet among the rabble who rained down on her, could be found none who met Audrey's blueprint for a suitable custodian of the manor. This only strengthened her resolve to raise the money and buy it back herself.

But the arrival of these monied people also brought home to her the relative strengths of her own resources, and that of the competition. Yet she persisted in her fund-raising efforts in a style of which Horatio Bottomley would have been proud. This had to be done in the time between viewings. People ebbed and flowed to such an extent that she was grateful when she was left alone, or at least with people she trusted. Her whole circle of acquaintance was now dividing into 'those for' and 'those against'.

Her two closest aides among 'those for' were Marjory her old school friend and Brabinger the butler. Of course, all Audrey needed at this crisis in her life was somebody to say 'yes' and 'no' at the appropriate junctures. At this Brabinger, as befitted his vocation, excelled. In the course of a butler's duties, there is little enough to say, but Brabinger's repertoire of 'yesses' and 'noes' and 'indubitablies' were capable of so many modes of expression, that he could pass himself off as a most colourful conversationalist.

Sometime later in the day, Audrey would tire of her brave-face act, and adopt a more true-to-life death cell expression. Only Brabinger was privy to this. He would bring her her evening coffee, and then would talk for a while. It became clear from these conversations that in her heart she knew she was done for. Curious though, that it was Brabinger to whom she was confiding — albeit unconsciously. In fact, she was determined to detain him on some pretext — and pretexts to indulge in nostalgia were not difficult to come upon, surrounded as she often was with trunks and boxes of memorabilia which were being brought up from the cellar.

'Look at this, Brabinger,' she said one evening, handing

34

him a sepia photograph. 'That's *you*, isn't it?' It was indeed. It was a staff photograph dated 1919.

'Bless my pants, so it is,' said Brabinger. 'I was a mere stable lad then.'

'Thought you'd be amused.'

'Do you know, madam, in those days it was my job to mark out the family crest in sand in the stable yard every morning. And the Latin family motto.'

'Huh,' said Audrey, 'I thought mottos were to give one moral strength in times of crisis.'

'Indeed, madam.'

Audrey read the Latin.

' "I will give up my life",' Brabinger translated. 'I've always thought there's something very incomplete about it. There must be a more positive bit somewhere — probably got knocked off the coat-of-arms by Cromwell.'

Audrey wasn't listening. She wasn't detaining him to hear *his* opinions.

'What's wrong with the cook?' she asked, scrutinizing the photograph. 'She's all fuzzy.'

'She had a nervous twitch. That photo was taken on an old 1891 Lancaster — it had a sixteen-second cap exposure, while the cook had a twelve-second twitch.'

'How quaint,' said Audrey, off-handedly. 'Oh, look, here's one of me and Marton.'

The photograph she showed him was of a weekend picnic party in the forties. In the foreground was a little girl with ringlets and a boy pulling at her ribbons.

'Oh, yes, madam — I remember that well. The week-end house party for the Duke of Aldershot and the Marchioness of Dartford. They were most discreet.'

'What do you mean, "discreet", Brabinger? Do you mean that they were...' she gestured that the two parties knew each other rather better than their separate titles suggestd they ought.

'Indeed, madam.'

'Do you mean the manor was being used as a house of assignation for an affair *à la main gauche*?'

'You could put it like that, madam,' he agreed.

'Well, I never realized. I'm appalled.'

She looked at the photograph again. 'Doesn't Mrs Beavis look like thunder?'

'The governess, God rest her. That was the day you locked her in the oubliette.'

'Fancy you remembering that.'

'I was with her, madam.'

'So you were. Well — it was Marton's idea, not mine.'

'We didn't blame you for an instant, madam.'

'Isn't this the picnic when Aunt Bertha fell out of the rumble seat of the car?'

'The old seventy-horse Napier, madam, yes. Never forget that day. Forty people including the twelve staff, sixty bottles of wine — and no corkscrew. Remember, I had to go back to the manor to get one.'

'What a memory.'

'It was the first time I had ever driven the Rolls, ma'am. And there was also that incident of your cousin Peverell and the hornet.'

'And Uncle Lancelot setting fire to his night-shirt. Remember?'

'I do, madam. I remember it well.'

'Still, I suppose it did get rid of his hiccoughs.'

They laughed.

And so those late-night conversations went on, occasioned by the flimsiest excuses, as Audrey went through her family boxes full of family trees and genealogies, blacksmith bills, clockwinder's instructions, Breeches Bible, bundles of letters written in elegant copper-plate up and down the pages as well as across it, old medals, military citations — so it went on. At times, so engrossed was Audrey in both the past and the future, that she was oblivious of the present, and scarcely aware of there being anybody else in the room. As the conversation tended to be one way, it didn't matter who it was, and Brabinger and Marjory took it in turns to be with her.

Marjory could be reliably counted among 'those for'. She was always popping in, claiming that the manor was 'on her way', though why it should be on her route between her own cottage a mile away and Marlbury, three miles in the opposite direction, nobody ever enquired.

She had always been a familiar face in the manor, and had familiarized it even more since Marton had died. She was acting in her capacity as friend, and was being what is known as a brick, that is to say, better for building houses with than dispensing balm and comfort. Yet she had a heart as big as a bucket, and the best will in the world, if not the county.

She had always looked in to see how Audrey was coping. Usually she just marched in when she felt like it, but sometimes she had a formal invitation. One particular night it was for dinner, and Marjory had gone to the trouble to dress up for it, and was wearing a white made-to-measure creation, but whoever it was made-to-measure, it certainly wasn't Marjory.

She was now standing in the hall, wondering where Audrey might be, when a sound from the drawing room disclosed her whereabouts.

'Yes, Arnold, I heard. Manchester,' she went on. 'I know we have some relatives in far-flung parts of the world, but really — Manchester.... Well, I suppose ten thousand pounds isn't to be sniffed at. What does the man do? Heir to *what* roller-towel fortune?'

Audrey was either talking to somebody with a very faint voice, or she was on the phone.

Marjory was notorious for getting the wrong end of sticks, but in gathering from her half of the conversation that Audrey was talking to Arnold, her solicitor who was informing her that progress had been made in persuading relatives to stump up with the funds — she was right.

It seemed the relatives were beginning to cough up, albeit polite coughing, they were not choking themselves to death yet; but who knows — the full-blown bronchial hack might follow, and when that happened, Audrey would certainly be ready with the spitoon.

'I don't care whether the money comes from Hottentots or Matabele warriors,' Audrey was saying heatedly, 'so long as they're family and have the wherewithall under their belts....' She heard a chuckle on the other end of the line.

'No need to be vulgar, Arnold.' She motioned Marjory in to sit down. Marjory had already done so.

'What about the mineral money?' she was saying. 'Uncle Gussy's illegitimate branch. Find them, Arnold. Round them up. Good-bye.'

'You make your relatives sound like sheep.'

'In intelligence, yes. But they don't seem to have the herd instinct I would have expected. Still, we've got a certain amount out of them. It's a start.'

'Have you found out much?' asked Marjory, indicating the chaos all around her.

'There are far more of us than I thought,' said Audrey, picking up the family tree. 'Of course, they wouldn't qualify under normal circumstances, but these aren't normal circumstances. I've been turning out the archives for clues. Hence the mess.'

'Mess? I thought the place looked rather tidy. Almost bare. What have you done?'

'Oh, I've taken all the 'In Sympathy' cards down. Pity, they made the place look so cheerful. I've left Mrs Beacham's up. It's priceless.'

She took the card down — it was a purple wreath. She read it.

'May me and Harry offer you every assistance with your death.'

They laughed.

'Dear Mrs Beacham,' said Audrey as she put the card back on the mantelpiece. 'Been with us forty years and I've never once had to mark the gin bottle.'

Marjory had been doing some thinking and she was being more of a realist. She felt that Audrey, in her quest for a million, was flying kites. She had been meaning to make Audrey see sense, but on three previous occasions, when the subject came up, her nerve failed her at the last minute.

'Audrey, why don't you settle for what you've got? You're turning down a golden opportunity to start a new life. You could remarry even.'

Audrey retaliated like a startled rattlesnake.

'Have you been talking to Arnold?' she hissed. 'Are you two in cahoots? He's been trying to persuade me to leave here and sit bottling fruit until Mr Right comes along. Well, no thank you. Unless of course, it turns out to be a Mr Rothschild.'

'All you talk about is money. There are other things besides money.'

'Yes, there are stocks and shares, mortgages, deeds, bonds,' she said, flinging scrolls and certificates into the air.

'No,' said Marjory sharply, feeling her blood boil, 'there are things like romance to consider.'

'You mean sex — you're sex mad. I could get anything I wanted in that line just by snapping my fingers.'

'I've never found snapping my fingers that exciting,' said Marjory.

'You all over-rate it. It's unfortunate I know, but it happens to be the only way of continuing the line. It's no coincidence that 'bedroom' is an anagram of 'boredom'. No, the only reason to marry again now, is to stay at the manor. At best, it would be an arranged marriage, like it was with Marton.'

'Was that an arranged marriage?'

'Of course — I arranged it. Mind you, if I'd known he was going to peg out before the title blew his way....'

39

Marjory began to simmer again over this hot-plate of callousness.

'Oh, Audrey, you're getting very bitter. You're not yourself. Look, you should get away. At least you'd be spared having to watch prospective buyers traipsing through the manor.'

'I'm getting used to it.' said Audrey, casually resuming her rummaging.

'They're wasting their time. But I wish they wouldn't maul the tapestries and leave thumbprints all over the Waterford. The Arabs are the worst, then the Australians, then the Dutch and the Americans.'

'What are the English like?'

'I wouldn't know. There haven't been any yet. You know, that's strange,' she said wistfully. 'I thought that we'd get one or two, even if they're just looking. If I don't get the manor....'

'Aha,' blurted Marjory. 'So you admit that possibility.'

'I admit nothing. But if, but just if— I'd like it to go to an Englishman. "England for the English" as we used to say about India.'

Marjory's attention was caught by the sound of a footfall on the blue-lias stone in the hall. She also heard voices.

'Here comes another,' said Marjory.

'Let them come,' challenged Audrey with the same hauteur with which Marie Antoinette once said something about cake.

The door opened with a creak which might have been the turn of the handle or Brabinger who was attached to it. Bertie raced to the door, barking.

'Mr Anderson is back with another viewer,' proclaimed Brabinger.

'At this time of night?'

'He has an appointment.' The dog stopped barking. 'I gather he has motored from London, madam,' Brabinger went on.

'What is it this time? A pygmy chief?'

'British, I believe, madam.'

'Doctor Livingstone, I presume,' scoffed Audrey. 'Show them in.'

Anderson appeared in the doorway.

'And this is the lounge,' he was telling somebody.

'Yes, this is the drawing room,' corrected Audrey.

Anderson seemed surprised to see her.

'I'm so sorry to disturb you, Mrs fforbes-Hamilton, but I wonder if I might show Mr DeVere the...er...er...state rooms?'

The man hovering in the doorway came forward, revealing himself to be as described. He was wearing a pinstriped suit, a club tie, with a gold tie-pin, and a carnation in his buttonhole. His sartorial impact made Anderson, in his shapeless tweeds, look fit for a Guy Fawkes night bonfire. Bertie cowered away from him, growling, and began barking at the nearest vacant chair until silenced.

'Good evening, Mrs fforbes-Hamilton. I'm Richard DeVere. You may remember...'

'Yes, indeed I do,' gushed Audrey, her social training coming to the fore, and charging towards him with outstretched right hand and left elbow in the air. 'How good to see you again.'

'We met at your funeral,' said DeVere as he shook the limb out of self-defence as much as politeness.

'So we did.'

'Only this time I have an appointment.'

Audrey smiled.

'I didn't know you'd be interested in buying the manor, Mr DeVere.'

'Yes, I've decided to settle for a quieter lifestyle. Since my wife....'

'Passed away. Yes, you told me.'

'Grantleigh may be just the place for me,' he went on.

'Thank heavens. You've no idea some of the frightful

designs some of these foreigners have had on the place,' said Audrey. She scrutinized his city suit. 'You don't look like a farmer.'

He laughed.

'I'm not. I'd like to dabble in a bit of farming, though.'

'I see, so you intend to just live here and dabble?' Audrey asked with a hint of sarcasm.

'Yes and no.'

'You're very versatile, Mr DeVere. What do you mean?'

'I don't think this is the place to go into it. Let's just say I have plans.'

'You may speak freely.'

'Well, I was thinking of moving my business here.'

'Business?' Audrey didn't like the sound of this. She looked to Marjory for reassurance, but she was mesmerized by this vision of sartorial elegance which stood before her. 'What sort of business?'

'I'm in foods.'

'We mostly grow our own here — there wouldn't be much demand.'

'I own supermarkets.'

'I'm sure we already have a supermarket — whatever that is.'

'It's an international operation, run on a telex link, so it doesn't matter if it's run from here or Timbuctu.'

'I'm sure there are some delightful properties on the market in Timbuctu,' Audrey suggested.

'Ah, but not within hopping distance of London and Paris.'

DeVere said this with such conviction and emphasis that she realized that he had thought his motives out and meant business. It grieved her that of all the wonderful virtues and advantages which Grantleigh offered, its position, its beauty and history, they should all be relegated down a peg by the single fact of being within hopping distance of London and Paris.

'I don't think I need say more,' DeVere said.

'On the contrary, I'm most interested.'

'No, it would be churlish of me to talk of a future of this estate of which you would clearly not be part. I mean, the circumstances of this sale can't be everything you might want.'

'They're not, but I can take it. A strong umbrella does for hailstones as well as for light drizzle,' said Audrey.

'If you insist I tell you, it's my intention to move my headquarters here and perhaps use the manor as a leisure centre for some of my business associates.'

Audrey cringed. Her metaphorical umbrella buckled under the weight of this downpour.

'Do I take it that you plan to turn Grantleigh into some kind of gastronomic Disneyland?'

Anderson, never one to be left out of a conversation irrespective of the quality or tact of his personal contribution, felt obliged to pitch in.

'We have been discussing a most interesting plan to turn the ballroom into an office concourse, and the study into a wire-room. Oh, and the gun-room would make an excellent sauna bath, we thought.'

Audrey felt faint. DeVere sensed her discomfort and silenced the agent with a stony look.

'Shall we proceed with our tour, Mr Anderson? Good evening, Mrs fforbes-Hamilton,' he said with a disarming grace. 'I'm sorry to have disturbed you.'

He moved off towards the door, but Audrey called him back.

'You're not one of the Staffordshire DeVeres, are you?'

'No — I managed without.'

'I thought not. Good-bye.'

The two men stepped into the darkness of the hall, guided by the sound of Brabinger wheezing. The sound of footfall on blue-lias faded.

Marjory was still standing agape at the space where her

new found inamorato had just vacated.

'Well, really,' Audrey spluttered.

'A leisure centre, indeed — that's the worst idea yet. Just imagine it, Marjory.'

Marjory was still mesmerized and didn't flinch.

'Marjory!'

She flinched.

'Just imagine it.'

'I was.'

'Pinball machines in the great hall, Geisha girls in the conservatory. Whatever next? English that man may be, but there's something about him which isn't quite right.'

'I thought he was rather delicious.'

'I'm talking about his manner, not his gastronomic potential. The wrapping was fine, but somehow there was something wrong with the whole package. What was it?'

'The string?'

'I know,' said Audrey. 'He's nouveau.'

'How could you say such a terrible thing,' Marjory protested.

'He certainly isn't one of one. For a start he's trade. He can't be a gentleman and have a job. And besides, remember what Miss Archibald told us at school. Never trust a man who tucks his shirt inside his underpants and has creases in his sleeves.'

'How do you know about his underpants?'

'Intuition. But he certainly had creases in his sleeves.'

'And I suppose you're going to say next that he eats with his hat on.'

'How did you know, Marjory?'

'Intuition. Still, it's nice to find an Englishman with some money.'

'Money!' Audrey mocked. 'Now, who's obsessed with money? Money he may have, but the ability to run a historic estate is in the blood. It isn't something you can buy at Boots.'

Audrey launched into a little impersonation of DeVere shaking her head from side to side in the manner of smooth film characters, and affected his crushed-velvet voice.

' "I think I might dabble in a bit of farming." I mean to say, an activity which has kept fifteen families fully occupied for four hundred years can't be called "dabbling", can it? Can you really imagine that man as the lord of the manor of Grantleigh?'

'He might be rather good,' said Marjory, lapsing from her role as Audrey's yes-woman.

'Now, don't you be beguiled by those rugged good looks and the hair attractively greying at the temples, and that glib tongue of his...'

She realized that a crack was appearing in her mask of instant suspicion, and she was giving too much away. For a moment, Marjory could see that she was not alone in her sudden infatuation.

'He has nice eyes,' she said.

'So do camels,' snapped Audrey.

'But there's something fishy about him. Bertie skulked into the corner of the room, and she's always right about people, aren't you, my poppet?' she gushed, bearing down on the little creature who dived for cover under the cushions on the sofa.

'He's just not quite right. I can't help feeling he's like fish and chips wrapped in *The Times*. I wonder if he's in the *Who's Who*?'

Audrey bounded across the room to the secretaire bookcase, and fingered her way throught the leather-bound volumes which Marjory called the 'Snob Section'.

'Do you think he *is* somebody?' she said, using that loaded word.

'He must be *some*body.'

'I don't mean somebody somebody. I mean somebody *somebody*. Or even some*thing* somebody-somebody. I mean as opposed to anybody.'

'Oh yes, he must be opposed to anybody,' agreed Marjory, trying to untie the semantic granny-knot.

Audrey had found the 'Ds'.

'Is it a little d and a big V, or a big D and a little v, or a big V and a big D? And will it be under V or D? ... Ah, here it is.'

She continued to mumble to herself.

'Ah, here are the Staffordshire DeVeres. Oh, and there appears to be some Suffolk ones I didn't know about. No,' she said at length, slamming the book shut in a cloud of dust, 'no Richard DeVere. Perhaps he's changed his name from something. Now why should he change his name?'

'Perhaps he's so important he's ex-directory,' dared Marjory.

'Marjory, the Queen is in here,' she barked, waving the book under Marjory's nose. 'These aren't the Yellow Pages, you know.'

Marjory took her point.

'I wonder if the Queeen is in the Yellow Pages,' she mused.

'What would she be under? Bridge openers?'

'Monarchs, maybe.'

'How about under "ship-launchers".'

'Parliament-openers?'

The two friends were laughing as Brabinger appeared at the door.

'Dinner will be served in half an hour, madam.'

'Glory, I had no idea it was so late. Excuse me, Marjory, I must go and change.'

She looked at herself in the mirror for justification of this course of action. Then she looked at Marjory with particular attention to her turn-out.

'Don't you dress for dinner any more?'

'I have,' Marjory confessed.

'To cook it or eat it?'

With that, Audrey scooped Bertie off the sofa with a

'come along, darling, din dins,' and left the room.

The Trust Fund now stood at what Arnold called 'a lot of beans'. Audrey did not want to know the details, suffice it to know that the trust was now in a position to make a substantial bid come the auction. Pledges were coming from all over the place, most of them conditional on proof of other covenants being honoured and a minimum sum being raised.

Audrey had stopped asking where the money was coming from, as it was fairly obvious that the concept of family was beginning to show stretch marks. It now included pension funds and insurance and investment companies, whom Arnold referred to as 'distant aunts'.

If the litmus test of kinship were applied, it figured that in any organization which employed a lot of people, there might be a blood relative working for it somewhere. Were we not all sons of Adam? What appealed to the investors, who could no doubt find better short-term returns for their money elsewhere, was that this money was being invested in a rapidly diminishing commodity and therefore increasingly valuable, land. It would be a long-term investment, but what appealed to them in the short term was that here was a fight to keep feudal England both English and feudal.

Audrey had sentiment on her side. Uncertain as to whether the preservation of the feudal system was good or bad, investors were giving her the benefit of the doubt. The fund swelled.

Things seemed to be going very well, yet Audrey remained certain she would lose. However, the blessed Marjory stayed by her side and bore her taunts heroically.

She too had played her part in the fund-raising by organizing a jumble sale. After expenses had been accounted for, the Trust Fund owed the jumble sale £5. All there was to show for it was the dispersal of Marton's old clothes which Audrey had donated, but had regretted it once his suits and shirts started turning up all over the estate — mostly on Midianites, but once on a scarecrow. Combining elements of both was Ned, the factotum, who chose to wear his former master's tails to the auction itself, for at last, that dreaded day was upon them.

It was ten to three. Marjory was watching the arrivals in the forecourt from Audrey's bedroom window, and relaying their identities to Audrey who was getting ready. She saw the limousines draw up and being parked to the specification of the Constable Peaslake.

It was now clear from Peaslake's jubilant manner, that he was relishing this day. Like '47, whatever it was that happened, this year would engrave itself in his memory as the day Grantleigh changed hands, and he now seemed to be welcoming the arriving parties as saviours who were to deliver the estate from tyranny.

As one would expect, his spirits were in marked contrast to Audrey's — who, considering the circumstances and her foreboding of doom, was remarkably calm. It was the waiting and uncertainty which had been making life unbearable. For better or worse, that bit was nearly over. To Marjory's surprise, as Audrey waited in her room, she seemed less concerned with the imminent auction than with frivolous trifles. Her primary preoccupaton seemed to be what one wore for auctions.

'Is there such a thing as correct auction wear?' she said. 'I wonder what the well-dressed bidder is wearing this year?'

Even if Marjory had an answer, it was too late to act on it. She was dressed.

'Are you ready, dear?' said Marjory, who was looking down into the forecourt where Midianites were now arriving.

'Just a minute,' Audrey baulked. She was looking at her signet ring. 'No, I don't think I ought to wear this. It might

48

bring me bad luck.'

'What?'

'This ring — it's got the family motto on it.'

She read the Latin.

'I will give up my life,' translated Marjory.

'In other words, "I will give my all", and I'm blowed if I'm going to give up one scrap of it.'

She wrested it from her finger, and put it on the dressing table.

There was a knock at the door.

'It is nearly three, madam,' came Brabinger's voice.

She left her bedroom and walked along the gallery, with the trepidation which Charles I might have experienced on the way to the scaffold. As she appeared at the gallery, the groundswell of conversation abated, faces looked up at her from the well of the hall. A hush fell on the great hall, and all eyes followed her as she made her way down the central stairway with Brabinger holding her arm. On the halflanding Brabinger began to tire, and she helped him down the rest of the way. In the sea of faces before her, she looked in vain for just one she recognized, among the range of tinted pigments arrayed before her like the gloomy end of a paintshop colour spectrum.

At the bottom of the staircase, a platform had been built, and a table placed on it, behind which grim-faced officials and the bank's solicitors sat shuffling their papers. Among them was Julian Anderson. In front of this were rows of seats. Audrey took her place between Marjory and Arnold, who was nervously paring his nails.

'What are our chances?' Audrey asked him.

'Difficult to say,' he replied.

'What's the total?'

He whispered in her ear.

'Good God!'

For a moment, she harboured hope, but it was soon dispelled when she looked round to see the rows of monied

49

people. Now she began to pick out faces she knew — old Ned, the rector, the clock. The latter struck three.

'Ask not for whom the bells tolls. It tolls for me,' she said lugubriously.

'Oh, don't be dramatic,' Marjory urged her.

'I am about to lose my home — you can hardly expect me to be out on the lawn playing croquet. Who are all these people?'

She looked around again at the assembly, picking out persons who, by virtue of their dress, beard-arrangements or just non-Englishness, were undoubtedly foreign.

'Where are all the English people with money to spend?'

'Ireland, Jersey or Switzerland if they've got any sense,' said Arnold laughing. Audrey glared at him. She looked at a group of Arabs in djellibas and burnouse and listened to the rattling worry-beads.

'If we're not careful, we'll find this house is going to be rebuilt brick by brick in Abu Dhabi. Look at them all.'

'Like vultures round a honey pot,' added Marjory for colour.

'Vultures don't like honey,' Audrey reminded her coldly.

The rector appeared at the end of the row. 'Good luck,' he said.

'What are you doing here, rector? Are you representing the church commissioners?'

'Simply offering my pastoral services at this time of trial.'

'It's an auction, not a trial.'

'A figure of speech. I am simply doing the Lord's bidding.'

'Oh,' mocked Audrey, 'I didn't know He was interested. Even that would be something. At least He's English.'

A gavel sounded, and everybody looked towards the platform. Anderson was standing up.

'Good afternoon, ladies and gentlemen,' he said in a loud voice which echoed off the ceiling. 'It's after three o'clock, so we ought to start.'

The chatter subsided.

'Hold my hand, Marjory. I think I'm going to die.'

Anderson was welcoming the present company to Grantleigh as if it were his own, and was extolling the virtues of his firm, which he said had been instructed to sell the property.

'Dispose' of, was the word he used, which grated on Audrey's nerve-endings like squeaking blackboard chalk.

The estate agent then included a disquisition he could well have left out to spare her feelings: he gave a full account of Marton's bankruptcy and the circumstances under which the manor was possessed by the bank. He then gave a colourful description of the manor, the dimensions in acres and hectares and drainage rights, and gave a lengthy appraisal of its production potential. How anyone could have made a loss out of it escaped him altogether, but he was at pains to point out that it had nevertheless been done. There followed a lot of references to 'subject to reserve', 'cognisance of conditions', and so on, and then at last he said, 'So now I invite bids. Will anybody start?'

Nobody would.

'Then who will give me seven hundred and fifty thousand pounds?'

'Lord love us,' said Audrey, raising her brochure to her head.

'Was that a bid?' inquired Anderson.

'Not yet.'

Arnold and Marjory constrained her. There was no bid.

'Who will give me seven hundred thousand?'

An Arab nodded and waved his brochure.

'Thank you, sir. Do I hear seven fifty?'

A brochure flashed at the back. Anderson accepted it and wrote the bid down.

'I'm offered seven hundred and fifty thousand. Do I hear eight hundred?'

He did. The bidding suddenly took off and the price shot

up to £850,000. Arnold had not yet made a move.

'Who will give me nine hundred?' said Anderson briskly.

There was silence.

'Then I'll offer it at eight hundred and fifty thousand pounds to the gentleman in the towel. For the first time.'

He raised the gavel and looked around the hall. Audrey could contain herself no longer.

'Eight hundred and fifty-five thousand.'

'Thank you, madam.'

'Not yet,' whispered Arnold.

'Eight hundred and sixty,' came a epiglottic Japanese voice.

'Any more bids?'

'Eight seventy,' yelled Audrey, ignoring Arnold's constraints. She looked round the hall, daring anybody to top her bid. It was then she noticed that DeVere, the one Englishman she thought was in competition, wasn't there. Where was he? She was already bidding beyond her means.

'Eight seventy-five,' came a mid-European voice.

'And 50p,' said Audrey.

There was laughter. Audrey glowered and looked round to see a man with a red carnation slip in at the back.

'Eight seventy-six,' he shouted.

'Then I'll offer it at eight hundred and seventy-six thousand pounds,' said Anderson. 'It's your bid, sir, at the back of the hall in the red carnation. I'm selling the property for the first time...'

Audrey was straining at an emotional leash but could do nothing. She was in something between a stupor and a coma, but at all events, dumbstruck.

'For the second time ... sold.'

He banged the gavel. A heavy sigh, along with the protests from pipped bidders, went up from the hall as tension was relieved and there was much shuffling of feet and coughing.

Audrey tried to stand up, groaned, and slumped back in

her seat again, her hand to her head.

'What happened?'

'We lost.'

'Is that *it*? I mean, it was so quick — can't we have it again? I wasn't ready.'

'It's too late,' said Arnold, 'we were beaten — and fairly — and that's that.'

'Who by?'

Anderson was still talking.

'If the gentleman in the red carnation would like to come forward and sign the memorandum and pay the deposit.'

Richard DeVere was already well on his way to the rostrum. In fact, he was level with Audrey's row of chairs, and Audrey could see him being congratulated by some of the other losers on his way.

'Oh, thank heaven,' sighed Audrey, with evident relief when she saw who it was. 'He's English.'

The rector passed by again.

'Say not the struggle naught availeth,' he said, by way of comfort.

'I wasn't going to,' said Audrey archly, 'not that it appears to have availed in the least.' She got up. 'Well, that's it, isn't it? So quick, so clinical, so brutal.'

Marjory stammered her condolences.

'I'm sorry, dear,' she almost sobbed, 'you must be brave.'

'Cheer up, Marjory. That's only one possibility gone out of the window. There are others.'

'What do you mean?'

'So much for contingency plan A.'

Arnold raised his eyebrows, and looked at Marjory.

'Do you know what you are going to do now?' he asked.

'Of course — move on to contingency plan B. Excuse me.' She forced her way between them, moving towards the platform.

Marjory stopped her.

53

'I hope this isn't one of your wild ideas,' she said.

'No — it's one of yours, actually. You remember you and Arnold saying that I should go and live somewhere else?'

'Yes,' they chorused.

'And wait for someone to come along?'

'You mean, Mr Right?'

'Well, perhaps not Mr Right — but I think I've just met Mr Convenient!'

She was looking at DeVere, who stood out head and shoulders above the cluster of people on the platform. They followed her gaze, and then looked back at her in amazement.

'Audrey,' gasped Marjory, 'You're not thinking of...?'

'Why not? He's English — and besides, I think he's rather delicious.'

She brushed past them and strode up to the platform.

DeVere was now bent over the table with his chequebook open, being pressed to sign a cheque for a deposit of £87,600.

'Congratulations, Mr DeVere,' said Audrey behind him.

He turned and saw her holding out her hand. He shook it.

'Thank you, Mrs fforbes-Hamilton. I'm sorry it had to happen this way.'

'Somebody had to win, somebody had to lose.'

'This may not be the time to discuss it — but I do have plans, and if you're willing, they could include you.'

'Gracious. How thoughtful.'

'So, Mrs fforbes-Hamilton...'

'Call me Audrey.'

Anderson was tugging at DeVere's sleeve like a little child.

'The cheque,' he was saying. 'Could you sign the cheque?'

DeVere signed the cheque with impatience, and turned back to Audrey. Audrey felt this was the moment to deliver

54

her prepared speech.

'I want you to know that I am very glad that it is you who has bought Grantleigh. I think it is so important that England should remain in the hands of the British, don't you?'

'That is one view, yes' he said, a noticeable element of doubt in his voice.

'Excuse me,' said Anderson, butting in, looking at the cheque with bewilderment, 'but who is Bedrich Polouvička? Is that you, sir?'

'Yes,' said DeVere, pocketing his gold pen.

'I see, a pseudonym?'

'No,' said DeVere candidly, 'it is my real name.'

'What?' gasped Audrey.

'It's my real name,' DeVere admitted. 'Richard DeVere is my English name. My real name is Bedrich Polouvička.'

Audrey turned white.

'One of the Bratislava Polouvičkas,' he went on, returning his chequebook to his pocket.

'But, you're ... you're ... so English,' she said, 'I mean, you couldn't be ... foreign.'

'Try me,' said DeVere.

3

'What's more he called me Audrey.'

'But you did ask him to, dear,' said Marjory.

'Yes, but that was before I knew he was foreign. I've never been called by my Christian name by a foreigner, let alone a Czechoslovakian.'

'And what's different about a Czechoslovakian?'

'I don't know. It's just that you don't know what to expect of a Czechoslovakian. He's not like, say, the Italians, the French, or Arabs or something where you know what to expect. Or even Spaniards.'

'What do you expect of Spaniards?'

'Almost anything — if they can build their capital city in the middle of a desert, they're capable of anything.'

'But you must admit he does speak the language well.'

'And so he should — he's been here long enough.'

It goes without saying that the speculation to-ing and fro-ing between Marjory and Audrey was on the subject of Richard DeVere, on whom they'd now been assembling information during the month since the sale. They knew, for instance, that he was not the born Briton he appeared to be, but that his appearance and manner and speech were acquired over the years. He had perfected them to a degree so that even the Audreys of this world could not distinguish them from the real thing.

It goes without saying that to Audrey, having hitched her star to his British wagon only to be made a fool of, she regarded him as a *bête noire*.

It goes without saying that as it was only a matter of hours before she was due to leave the manor for ever, this would be the time for her feelings of rancour and resentment, not to mention grief and anguish, to come to a head.

It goes without saying, she was not happy.

Considering so much was going without saying, an awful lot was being said.

The last month had been murder, and Audrey's only palliative to the pain of her humiliation and the sorrow of leaving Grantleigh was to keep busy. There was little to choose in the matter of what form that keeping busy should take. She had to get out of Grantleigh. After her discovery of the way she had been deceived, there was no way she could accept his offer to stay on, move into the old servants' wing, and carry on running the estate as if nothing had happened.

That's what DeVere had in mind. So, she had found a place to go and Arnold had arranged for its purchase. That was the easy bit. This left her with three weeks in which to obliterate all traces of the fforbes-Hamilton presence in the manor where they had been firmly entrenched. She was single-handedly to dismantle 400 years of the family's association with the estate, and then take all the evidence of it and reconstruct it in a house not a fraction of the size. It seemed an impossible task.

Nevertheless, she attempted it with impressive efficiency. She was always to be seen fluttering around the house with a clipboard and a roll of sticky labels marked 'wanted', 'not wanted', 'sell', 'throw out', which she placed on each item she came across according to the decisions she came to. She tried not to think about her future, but occasionally she caught an uninvited glimpse of her destiny — one in which the pawn-shop and the Distressed Gentlefolk Association kept figuring prominently. But the vision would fade as soon as something else claimed her attention, like answering the phone to enquiries about her successor, DeVere. Indeed, she was frequently asked to take bookings for his social life, engagements which were once hers.

In fact, DeVere's future seemed to be taking up as much of her time as her own, but she almost welcomed any excuse not to do anything by way of moving out.

In spite of her efficiency everything was left until the last minute, and the last minute, or rather the last hours were soon upon her. The manor was full of removal men bringing furniture from upstairs into the pantechnicon which was backed up to the front door. Audrey had worked out an order in which they were to be put into the van so that when she unpacked at her new house, the things that she wanted to hand would not be buried by the contents of the attic, hence she had put everything she valued most dearly into the drawing room which would be emptied last of all. Among these was an ormolu clock which stood on the mantelpiece. It said nine o'clock. Her deadline was mid-day, three hours hence. It was not the best of times to get a phone call from Lady Mortlake.

Lady Mortlake was a live-wire of the local pony club, but in many other matters, she was a very disconnected one. Unless it had a saddle on it, she wasn't all that interested. And somehow, the news of the sale had only just reached her.

'Oh, it does make me cross,' she ranted, when told the news.

'It doesn't do a lot for me, either,' claimed Audrey.

'But what will happen to the gymkhana?' The pony club gymkhana was the cause of a long-standing rivalry between these two gentlewomen. It had always been held at Grantleigh, though Celia Mortlake had always wanted to stage the event at nearby Harborough Hall, and Audrey had refused to let go and to alternate year by year.

In gushing her commiserations, Lady Mortlake was

58

inwardly cock-a-hoop that at last the gymkhana could move to what to her had always been its natural home. Yet she did sympathize, and felt slightly guilty in extracting this crumb of comfort for herself, from her friend's cataclysmic misfortune.

In spite of her not having anything to do with it, Audrey thought that Grantleigh was still the place for it, and advised Lady Mortlake accordingly.

'Of course, you can ask the new owner, Mr DeVere, but I can't vouch for his answer. You see, he's foreign.' This was an abrupt note on which the conversation ended.

'That word gives me the heebies every time I say it,' said Audrey, putting the phone down.

'Foreigner?' said Marjory.

'Yes, foreigners are all very well in their place, but why should it be my place?'

'But Mr DeVere is a British citizen.'

'In name, yes. But he's NOCD.

'Oh, definitely Not Our Class, Dear; he's classless,' Marjory insisted.

'Yes, but lower middle classless. That manner of his is all put on. I knew it the minute he visited the house and called the sofa a settee. It's bad enough having the place sold over my head under my nose, without having it bought by somebody who probably doesn't know the difference between an old manor house and a bus shelter.'

She was getting in a flap. She had three hours to go and was packing the trunks and tea chests which surrounded her.

'Oh, I hate packing at the best of times, and this isn't the best of times.'

'It's like school, isn't it?' Marjory reassured her. 'Do you remember packing at the end of the last term at the convent? That was very sad. I'll never forget saying good-bye to Mother Superior.'

'She cried so much, she looked like Lake Superior,'

laughed Audrey.

As she carried a pile of her favourite photographs from the piano to a tea chest, she caught sight of herself in the looking glass.

'Oh, Lor,' she said, 'I do look a fright. I must tidy myself up before I say good-bye to everybody. I'd hate them to see me like this — give them the satisfaction of thinking I'm going to seed.'

'You know,' said Marjory, changing the subject, 'I do think Lady Mortlake should have more consideration. As if you haven't got enough on your mind at the moment.'

'I agree. Even if she *is* a friend of Princess Anne. And she's not the only one who's been pestering me. I've had the Queen Bee of the Guides asking if their jamboree here will be affected. Then there was the rural council who should know better — asking me to ask Mr DeVere to judge the carnival beauty contest. Honestly, as if he'd know what to look for in a Miss Dairy Products. Can you manage that?'

Marjory had unhinged a mounted buffalo's head and was easing it down the wall.

'This is man's work, really,' she admitted. 'Where's Brabinger?'

'Clearing out Marton's study. He's a bit shaky this morning. His health isn't what it used to be, you know. Not that it ever was. You know how he gets anything that's going.'

'What's he picked up this time?'

'A billiard table.'

The door opened, and Brabinger shuffled in with a portrait of Marton, painted during his 'India phase'.

Audrey rushed to his assistance. 'Brabinger, you are not to lift heavy things.'

She relieved him of it.

'Sorry to hear about your back, Brabinger.'

'Thank you, madam. A leg fell off this morning, but I managed to screw it back on,' said the retainer, and

60

disappeared into the study.

'I wasn't talking about the billiard table,' said Marjory.

'Dear old Brabinger,' said Audrey, when he was out of earshot, which was anything beyond standing right beside her. 'He's being so helpful.'

'Such a change,' Marjory quibbled. 'I thought myself that he'd been getting above himself.'

'I know, I blame 'Upstairs, Downstairs' myself. Oh, don't pack that one.'

Marjory was wrapping a picture of Marton, and stopped.

'But it's of Marton,' she protested. 'Surely you'd like to think of him as he was?'

'No, I honestly prefer to think of him as he is.'

'But you're a widow — it's the done thing for widows...'

'Don't use that word, Marjory,' Audrey butted in. 'It makes me feel like a spider.'

'But you really ought.'

'Don't tell me what I ought. The past is the past.'

'Yes — and you and Marton were childhood sweethearts, don't forget that.'

'Yes, but I was far too young to know my own mind. It subsided into a marriage. Of course, it started off well enough with the wails of heart-broken boyfriends and my photo in *Country Life*. But you expect marriage to start off with a great ballyhoo and then boil down to nothing — it's like spinach.'

Marjory laughed. 'You don't mean it?'

'I do, now it's over. I refuse to surround myself with old pictures of Marton in India posing with the Nawab of Ranjipur with a smoking twelve-bore and his foot on a dead tiger.'

The study door opened, and Brabinger tottered in, burdened with more items from Marton's India collection.

'You are *not* to carry heavy things,' Audrey rebuked him. 'How many more times?' She rushed to his aid and relieved him of a tablelamp made out of a stuffed crocodile, an old

61

pair of field-glasses, some polo sticks, a Malacca cane and an elephant's foot umbrella stand — and there was plenty more where that came from.

Audrey looked at her armful.

'Oh, happy days,' she said, nostalgically. 'I had such a wonderful time when Marton was in India.'

'I didn't know you were in India.'

'No, I wasn't. He was, and I had a wonderful time here. Do look at this obscene thing.'

It wasn't that the light came out of its open mouth which worried her so much as where the wire leading to it went in.

'I wonder if it still works?'

She separated the crocodile lamp from the rest, found a wall-socket and plugged it in.

'I don't know how he managed to get all this stuff. He was only in the Indian diplomatic Corps two months. Indeed they had sent him home straight after the embarrassing incident at an Embassy reception. Serve him right,' said Audrey. 'Fancy going up to Nehru and telling him his coat was buttoned up on the girl's side.'

She threw the switch. Nothing happened. The crocodile stood on its plinth with the bulb in its mouth. Audrey went to the switch under the crocodile's tail, and switched it on. The bulb lit up.

'He shot this himself, you know.'

'It still seems to work all right,' said Marjory. Marjory did try Audrey's patience sometimes.

'Come along now, we're holding Brabinger up — now, one thing at a time, Brabinger,' she advised, handing him back a polo stick. 'Here, put everything in a chest.' One advantage of Marton having been in India was that for their supply of tea chests they were in clover.

'Poor Brabinger,' she said, when Brabinger had gone. 'At least that's one consolation. It will be ideal for Brabinger.'

'What will be.'

'Living in a smaller house. Even if there is only one

62

bathroom. One really ought to have two.'

'The Mortlakes have got six!' said Marjory.

'Yes, well, that's pure ostentation.'

Brabinger reappeared, still carrying his polo stick and announced that the removal men were ready to clear the room.

'Closing in for the kill, are they? Do they expect me to roll over and offer them my jugular?'

'I think they've just *had* tea, madam,' said Brabinger, cupping his ear.

Two men, one in a cap and white apron and one in purple overalls appeared at the door.

'What a very smart hat,' said Audrey, admiringly. The man in the white apron took his cap off and looked at it for signs of smartness.

Its removal was the effect Audrey required.

'Thank you. Now, before you start, I want to tell you that in this room there are some very old and valuable pieces. Now, I don't expect you to know a Hepplewhite table from a fablon view of the Lake District, but I want you to treat everything as if it was your own.'

She looked at them dubiously and added, 'Well, carefully, anyway.'

She motioned them to start by removing the Chesterfield, but, for the benefit of the men, she called it a settee.

'Right, Arthur. Hear what the lady said? What we call the "sofa" first.'

The two men hoisted it and juggled with it with a concentration and confidence which seemed to threaten everything else in the room.

'Your way a bit. Right, shifty-lefty, mind the door jamb. Tippy-tippy. Bit more. OK. Straight ahead.' They were clear of the door. 'Right, pacey, pacey.'

A perfectly controlled and executed exit — at no time did the sofa make contact with the building or contents.

'That's just a sofa to them,' said Audrey, when they had gone. 'But when I think of the famous and noble posteriors which have parked themselves in that in this very room over the years, it really hurts to see it go. It's the end of an era. When Marton was alive ...'

'It won't help to think about him at this time,' Marjory advised.

'Well, how can I help it, after what I saw in the workshops yesterday. The mechanic brazenly wiping a dipstick on Marton's old underpants. I distinctly saw the monogram.'

'I'm sure that brought back some happy memories,' said Marjory, sarcastically.

'No, it didn't, as a matter of fact. I admit they weren't all good memories. I mean, I can see Marton now, sitting on that sofa telling that ridiculous story about the master of the Beaufort who had to go to Lourdes to get his riding boots off. He thought it was terribly funny. But then his idea of fun was to go round the billiard table putting his hands under all the pockets and saying, "cough". I must say, I never really understood that. But I'm talking about the past, and we have to get out of here.'

The two of them resumed packing up in silence. The hush was broken by Marjory who had been waiting for just such an opportunity to broach a new subject.

'Didn't Mr DeVere say you could stay on here as long as you liked?'

'Yes, but I can't, can I? It isn't fair on Brabinger, so I've moved on to contingency plan C. You can't ask him to stay here and watch DeVere turn the place into an amusement arcade for foreigners or whatever. It would be more than he could stand.'

'But it won't be that bad.'

'It will. This time next year this place will look like a UNICEF Christmas card. I wouldn't mind so much if only the villain of the piece was one of one, but he just isn't.'

'I keep telling you, he's pleasant enough.'

'If only one could be sure. He strikes me as the sort of man who'd wear brown shoes with a dinner jacket, and he probably cuts his toenails in the bath. Now, you'd better stop me before I say something uncharitable.'

'Well, I thing he's rather a dish.'

'Then the sooner he's cooked and eaten, the better.' Audrey returned. 'No, don't bother your mind trying to think of nice things to say about him.'

Marjory tried another tack. 'You'd be much more sensible to stay on, you know, at least until the new place is ready.'

Audrey didn't agree. 'I'd rather live in a house with only one bathroom than stay here with somebody else's style and taste I'm bound to find offensive. I mean, can you see me living with bowls of china fruit and blue water in the loo?'

Audrey was working herself into a lather of hatred, which suggested to Marjory that she had better let the matter drop.

'There is only one thing to do,' said Audrey finally. 'Pack up quickly and get out of here before he gets here. Because, if I have to meet him, I shan't be responsible for my actions.'

But it was too late.

They heard voices in the hall. One was Brabinger's, and the other gave Audrey the horrors. It was DeVere's.

'Is she still here? I would have thought she'd be gone by now,' it was saying as it came nearer.

Audrey threw down her clipboard. 'Not wanted', 'too big', 'sell' labels fluttered about, landing on the wrong furniture. One marked 'throw out' landed on Marjory.

'This is the last straw! Honestly, you'd think he'd have the courtesy to let me go with dignity and honour. He's early.'

Her manner changed abruptly as the door opened and Brabinger bustled in in considerable confusion.

'Madam ...' he began.

'So I see, Brabinger,' DeVere was in the doorway.

'Mr DeVere,' she gushed, switching on to automatic pilot, flying towards him with the outstretched right hand and the raised left elbow. 'How lovely to see you. What a wonderful surprise.'

'Hello, Audrey,' said DeVere, putting down his two cases and shaking her hand. 'I'm sorry. I appear to be a bit early.'

'Just two and a half hours,' said Marjory sarcastically. Audrey silenced her.

'Never mind,' she said. 'It's the early bird that gets the worm, as we say in England.'

'But it's the late worm which survives,' quipped DeVere.

'I'm sure it does in your part of the world,' said Audrey, smiling politely, wondering where she fitted into this image.

'I hope I haven't interrupted your plans?'

'No, no — I was only going to spend my last few hours here brooding, perhaps reliving old memories, perhaps bidding a fond farewell to some of my old haunts, then I was going to slip away quite unnoticed except for the dozen or so people coming in at twelve to see me off.'

The conversation was interrupted by the reappearance of the two removal men, who were admiring their next burden — a secretaire cabinet.

'When did you last see one of these, Arthur?' said the one in the apron.

'Dunno. Not for yonks. Not in laburnam, anyway, and certainly not oystered like that.' They ran their fingers over the carvings.

'Just look at that marquetry and bantamwork.'

'Bleeding marvellous, isn't it? There's only one bloke who ever did ebony stringing like that.'

'It's a Grinling Gibbons,' suggested DeVere.

Audrey, who had been looking with amazement from one

removal man to the other, now had DeVere testing the flexibility of her neck muscles.

'The very same, sir,' said Arthur. 'I was just going to say the same.'

Bert was looking under the cabinet. 'Course, if it *is* a Grinling Gibbons, there'll be a mark on it.'

Audrey pitched in sternly.

'If there is a single mark on it, I'll sue your company for every penny it's got.'

The two men were galvanized into action by this rebuke, and moved so fast that the cabinet seemed to skip out of the room on its own, muttering 'shifty lefty' to itself.

'That's *my* family furniture — so you haven't bought it,' said Audrey. 'In case you're wondering.'

'It hadn't occured to me. I think you have the wrong impression of me. You know that I don't want you to go at all.'

Audrey looked at him suspiciously and changed the subject.

'Oh, how inhospitable I'm being. Would you like to go upstairs?'

'No, thank you.'

'Only if you do, there's one downstairs. Oh, and your cases. Brabinger!'

'No, no, don't trouble him,' said DeVere, 'I'll take them.'

'In this house, Brabinger takes the suitcases. You mustn't confuse him.'

Brabinger appeared at the door. Audrey pointed.

'Brabinger, Mr DeVere's suitcases.'

Brabinger made for them, but just as he was about to grasp the handles, Audrey swooped on to them and swept them away into the hall.

'Brabinger has a bad back — he's excused heavy lifting,' she explained, as she came back, brushing her hands.

'Audrey, I wonder if you and I could have a little talk?'

67

said DeVere.

'I'm sorry, I do have an awful lot to do — I knew it would be a mistake to cling on till the last minute like this.'

'Maybe it's just the time to discuss your plans.'

'I'd rather not.'

'So you're still intent on leaving?'

'Of course.'

From DeVere there now followed a full and frank account of his reasons for wanting Audrey to stay on. It was an almost impassioned appeal, reinforced by references to his wife, his mother, his other commitments and so on. There was work to be done, he hadn't wanted the place to be revolutionized and had wanted things to go on much as they always had. She was an essential part of that plan. In fact, its pivot. There was the social side, too, and the farming, about which he confessed deplorable ignorance. Audrey loved the sound of it all, but would not relent. To turn him down would be van-in to her. And did she not herself have plans?

'You and I could make a good team,' he was saying.

'I'm sure you know why it's out of the question.'

'I don't — I mean, you could have all the rooms you need in the house, everything would be laid on for you.'

'I'm sure it would, but no thank you.'

'Then *what* are you going to do?'

'That's my business, Mr DeVere.'

'Yes, I suppose it is. There's one other thing. If ever you need any help — money, anything like that ... I hope you'll always feel free ...'

'That sounds like charity.'

'It isn't — call it a business proposition.'

'I don't intend to end up as a mere digit on your payroll.'

'That's not at stake. If ever you change your mind....'

'I never change my mind.'

'That's true,' said Marjory, making her debut in the conversation which, on a stony glance from Audrey, also

68

became her farewell performance.

'I think this conversation has taken an unfortunate turn in the circumstances. I had wished to spend my last few moments in this house alone — I am going for a walk now. I'll be doing the Upper Spinney walk, Marjory, and I won't be going for the speed record — I'd be grateful if you'd carry on packing. I'll be back just before twelve, ready to leave. Good morning.'

She stalked off towards the door. It opened from the outside to admit a little old lady, who Audrey had never seen before. She had a most striking presence though she was tiny, old and wrinkled. You could see that she had been dark and beautiful, and from a face with its proud features, shone a pair of piercing bright eyes which sparkled and twinkled. She was slightly stooped, and was dressed in a black overcoat and walked with a stick.

'How much longer am I going to have to wait in the car, boy?' she demanded of DeVere, thumping her stick on the ground with the dull throbbing you'd expect from a rubber bung on parquet. The accent was thick, and Audrey assumed it to be Czechoslovakian.

'My mother,' said DeVere. Audrey was horrified. 'Mother, this is Audrey fforbes-Hamilton — Audrey, Mrs Polouvička.'

'How do you do?'

Audrey took the frail hand in hers where it lodged in her palm, like a bundle of loose clothespegs.

'Enchanted, my child.' She looked at her son, and then spoke to Audrey.

'You spend your whole life cooking and sewing and cleaning and washing to give the boy a good start, and all for what? To spend your old age waiting in a car.'

Audrey's dutiful laugh belied an undertone of anguish. A new element had now crept into her quandary. She had considered the implications of DeVere's living at the manor and the variables of a relationship with him, but hadn't

69

given the old lady a thought. The canopy of hope that his nationality could eventually be kept under wraps, fell in ruins about her there and then. So this was to be the new dowager Duchess of Grantleigh? She would be all right so long as she didn't speak. As its ghastly implications coursed through her mind, she fell silent, a hiatus which the old lady felt obliged to break.

'So this is the house, is it?' she looked about her.

'I hope you'll like it,' said Audrey.

'Well, it certainly beats waiting in the car,' she opined. Audrey scowled. Then she added, for DeVere's hearing, '...specially when the TV's not working. I'm missing a schools programme on Indian crop-rotation.' She turned to Audrey. 'I'm sorry, my dear, this must be a very pungent moment for you.'

'Poignant,' corrected DeVere.

'No, no,' suggested Audrey unctuously. 'I think you may have been right the first time. Excuse me.'

Audrey continued on her way out. She turned as she got to the door.

'By the way, Mr DeVere, the pony club gymkhana takes place here next month. Lady Mortlake will be in touch. She's a friend of Princess Anne.' And with that she vanished.

'Did I say something wrong?' said the old lady when she'd gone.

'You just put your big size 6½ in it,' said DeVere.

'Maybe she's upset about something.'

'Mother, she is leaving her home — she's been here most of her life.'

'And so have we.'

'We *chose* to. She didn't.'

'I thought she was staying here with us.'

He turned to Marjory. 'Any ideas how we can persuade her?'

Marjory shook her head. 'None. I wonder if you'd excuse

70

me now. I have the packing to do.'

Marjory left the room.

Mother and son were left together to take in their surroundings.

'Well now, not bad, eh?' said the old lady.

'From barrow boy in Petticoat Lane to this.'

'You've done very well for yourself, my boy.'

'And I haven't got on by being crossed by people like Audrey. People just don't turn me down like that,' said DeVere stupified. 'I'll talk to her alone. Wait here. I'll go and speak to her.'

'Straighten your tie,' ordered the old lady.

Audrey was walking across the fields behind the old coach house, past old Ned's cottage with his son's police motorcycle chattering outside, then over the long meadow towards the stream. She was in gumboots and carried a crummock, in the manner of royalty when striking bucolic poses for birthday photographs. She was in a world of her own and scarcely noticed the salute from old Ned who was hedging and ditching on Hardnips field. She came across a cow out of the field, and finding the electric fence on, by resting a piece of grass on and edging her hand nearer the wire until she felt a warm tingle. She then traced the fence to the control box, switched it off, opened the fence shooed the cow in and turned the electric fence on again. All this was done absently, and by instinct, for her thoughts were on other things.

Her world was now one of the past. The wild flowers she was picking were those she had picked thirty years before. The bridge across the stream was not of the wooden lattice pattern she could see now, the pinewood she could now smell, or the creaking of the spars she could now hear as she walked across.

Already they were memories. What she heard was not the

gargle of a woodpigeon or the babble of the stream, but the voices of children playing. One of them was hers. The other was Marton's.

From the parapet, she could almost see two small faces in the stream where the water cowered and shrank from the force of the current, and coiled and writhed in little pools.

The faces were clear — one was hers, her hair in ringlets — the other was Marton's. She took a shank of bracken from her bunch of wild flowers and tossed it into the river.

'Let's play poohsticks, Audrey,' said the boy.

'All right — get a stick. Here's one,' replied the girl.

'Bags be Pooh.'

'You're always Pooh, Mart. I'll be Pooh.'

'I'll be Eyeore, then. Ready, steady, go.'

There was a gentle splash.

'Come on, slowcoach — bung yours in.'

There was another splash, and the race was on — the first stick to appear the other side of the bridge. The two excited voices egged the sticks on, borne by the current, and four little feet rushed to the other side of the bridge.

'Come on, Eyeore. Eyeore for ever.'

'Pooh, Pooh, Pooh!'

'Here comes mine. Eyeore wins,' said the boy.

'You're Pooh.'

'I'm, not. I'm Eyeore and that's mine.'

'S'not. It's mine.'

'Mine. I won by a squillion miles.'

'Where's mine then?'

'Got caught in the weeds.' They looked down. So it had. The boy laughed.

'Don't be rotten, Mart. That game wasn't fair. I wasn't ready.'

'All right, then — find another poohstick and I'll race you back.'

'My way this time,' said the girl.

'What way?'

'Against the current.'

Richard DeVere was out looking for her and, on Marjory's directions, was doing the Upper Spinney walk. He looked as far as he could along the footpath ahead of him but couldn't see her. But he could see Ned.

Yes, Ned had said lighting his pipe, she had passed a few minutes ago.

'Thank you,' said DeVere.

'Nice day,' said Ned, anxious to detain him.

'Yes, isn't it?' It was. It was very still.

'Still, reckon there'll be a storm tonight.'

'How do you know? The clouds, bird formations, wind direction or can you light a pipe without shielding the match?'

'It were on the weather forecast this morning, sir. You be from Lunnon, sir?'

'That's right.'

'I went there once. Never took to it, sir. All the traffic, the people jostling one another, and the noise and the shouting and the foreigners and the filthy air. Can't cross a road without getting run down. Never again, sir.'

'When was that?'

'Let me see now. Must be 1947.'

DeVere left Ned to his memories and walked on up the path. He passed the cow field with the electric fence, and there was still no sign of Audrey. He came to the stream and followed it as instructed, and then in the distance he saw her on the bridge.

As soon he came closer, he could see she was looking absently into the water. A thought occurred to him and, spurred by a sensation of pending disaster, he put his head down and strode faster along the path. When he raised his head again, she was gone. He ran to the bridge, expecting to see a *tableau vivant* of Millais' 'Ophelia'. There was no sign of her.

'Audrey, Audrey — where are you?'

'Be with you in a moment, Eyeore,' Audrey said calmly from behind a bush.

She appeared as advertised, holding a bundle of sticks.

'Oh, it's you, Piglet,' she said absently. 'I mean, Mr DeVere.' She awoke to her surroundings. 'I'm sorry, I was miles away.'

'Are you all right?'

'Of course. Why shouldn't I be?'

'I thought....'

He mimed a suicide plunge.

'Good gracious, no. Now, why should I do that? — and in three inches of water!'

DeVere felt a complete fool...

'No — I was just playing poohsticks.'

...but at least he seemed to be in good company.

'It's a game played by English children.'

'You're playing games at a time like this?'

'Yes.'

'Aren't you treating things a bit lightly?'

'We learn to take our defeats philosophically, Mr DeVere.'

'Perhaps we could call this a draw.'

'I know what you're implying, but my mind is made up. Now, come along.' She handed him a stick. 'You be Pooh — now, ready, steady, go.'

DeVere stood looking at his stick with embarrassment. Audrey grabbed it, hurled it into the stream, and raced to the other side of the bridge. DeVere, with his professional facility for grasping facts, worked out the rules for himself. Audrey's stick got caught up in the reeds.

'That's too bad,' said DeVere. 'Yours got caught up.'

'How dare you,' barked Audrey. 'That was yours!'

Anger seethed. 'That's just typical — not only do you come here to take my home, and arrive hours early to gloat

74

over me being pitch-forked into oblivion, but you also cheat at poohsticks.'

'But fair's fair,' protested DeVere. 'That was my...' the words jarred '...poohstick.'

A memory of some childhood injustice possessed her, and she wanted to cry. She fought it.

'What do you know about it? To think that this estate has fallen into the hands of a man who hasn't even heard of *Winnie the Pooh*.'

'Does it matter?'

'Of course it does,' choked Audrey. 'And what, may I ask, are you doing here, anyway? You're trespassing on a private estate which is my property for another three quarters of an hour ... well, my bank's, anyway. You might at least have kept your distance until I've gone.'

'I'm sorry,' said DeVere, chastened. 'I know how you feel.'

'How could you? You've never had anybody turf you out of your home, have you?'

'Not since Czechoslovakia in 1939, no.'

'Oh.' Now Audrey was sorry.

'But I'm British citizen now,' he went on.

'So you may be,' said Audrey, 'but that doesn't mean you're capable of running a Young Conservative ball.'

'I used to be a Young Socialist — I'm sure it's much the same.'

'I shouldn't have asked — all right then, what do you know about flower shows, shire horse parades, gymkhanas, and sheep-dog trials?'

'You have all those here?'

'Yes, and ploughing contests, have done since time immemorial. What's more, they will continue to be held here.'

Audrey was finding herself unaccountably eloquent and unabashed, and gradually she poured out her fears and misgivings.

'You have not just bought a piece of land and a few buildings,' she went on, 'you have bought a piece of history. There is no reason why history should stop with you. You don't own anything here any more than we did. It is simply in trust for your lifetime. I am merely entrusting you with the estate, and you're responsible for the continuance of its heritage, its traditions, its customs...'

'Oh.'

'...and the Marlbury Point-to-Point.'

They walked off the bridge and began to cross Hardnips field, as good a place as any to mention the Midianites. Audrey did so, pointing out that he was responsible for their welfare.

'It's called *noblesse oblige*. It's an English expression so I can't expect you to have heard of it. Oh, yes, they come to me with their personal problems, too. Only yesterday, Linda Cartwright came to me in tears with her lovelife. I'm not surprised since her boyfriend's idea of a courtship is going ferreting every Saturday afternoon. What's wrong with exercising the horses, I'd like to know.'

'I see. Anything else?' asked DeVere.

'I've hardly started. I think you should be acquainted with your duties as the new lord of the manor.'

'Lord of the manor?'

'It's just a name. It doesn't give you the right to the virginity of the gamekeeper's twin daughters.'

'*Droit de Seigneur*.'

She fixed him with a quizzical gaze.

'A Czechoslovakian expression,' he explained.

'You're too late, anyway. Which reminds me, you'll probably be required to take my place on the committee of the local adoption society. We are rotating members.'

DeVere smiled.

'It's not funny. And there's the unmarried mothers' club. You'll be expected to work for that.'

'What as? Recruiting officer?'

'That's not funny either. It has to be taken very seriously, and all you get out of all this hard work is the pick of the holly with the best berries on it at Christmas.'

They were passing the lake.

'By the way, the lake needs draining. It's full of stolen supermarket baskets which the Midianites keep dumping.'

'You don't think I'll let you down, do you?'

'It's a question of whether you're up to a job you're not bred to. People like you retire to the country expecting the easy life. You think that all we do in the country is spend our time sucking straw and teaching hedgehogs the highway code.'

DeVere was playing it cool.

'I must admit it's lovely here — you've no idea how refreshing it is to be in a place where everything smells sweet.'

'I read somewhere that that is one of the first symptoms of bubonic plague,' Audrey paused. 'It makes sense somehow.'

DeVere would not be brow-beaten, though what she had said certainly struck home.

'I think you'd be pleasantly surprised at how the place shapes up. I may come from the town, but I'm no fool.'

'I have·a good mind to stay and see that you do right by it.'

DeVere felt he was getting through to her.

They were passing Long Meadow from which the Home Farm herd stared at them.

'Look at that,' said DeVere. 'That bull. All the cows he wants in that field, and he's eating?'

'Don't be vulgar. This is a farm. It is no place for barnyard banter. That's the sort of thing you need somebody to put you right on. Yes, I've got a jolly good mind....'

Suddenly there came a loud mooing from behind them. They turned to see the cow which Audrey had once put back into the field.'

'If you're so capable, you can start by putting that cow back into the field.'

'You hardly need a box of brains to do that,' he said, as he slipped round behind the cow and shooed it back towards the fence.

'Cows can't jump,' screamed Audrey. 'You're thinking of frogs. The fence, the fence,' she cried, pointing.

DeVere played the perfect gentleman, albeit to a cow. He grabbed the fence in his palm and lifted it into the air, as if for the cow to pass under it. He shuddered as the electricity passed through him, but he didn't let go, nor did he utter a sound.

Audrey was both amused and impressed by this show of strength. DeVere pretended that nothing had happened. He eventually let go and trod the fence down, while Audrey rushed the cow over it.

'I can manage,' said DeVere.

Audrey was getting the measure of the man. Products of spartan public schools, moulded by cane, Dubbin, cold baths and Cascara Evacuant, couldn't have done that.

'That's what's bothering me,' she said. 'I'm beginning to think you can.'

As DeVere and Audrey walked across the Long Meadow, past the lodge and back to the manor, they discussed, guardedly, their own particular plans for the future. It was not a time of straight answers, nor indeed straight questions. The strain of this stilted, superficial conversation was becoming tiresome, and when they arrived at the manor they were glad to part company, DeVere on the pretext of settling his mother down somewhere, and Audrey, just wanting to be alone, going to her bedroom.

'Good Lord, is it nearly twelve o'clock?' said Brabinger,

prising himself out of a chair in the hall in which he had been dozing. He was wearing his chauffeur's uniform with epaulettes, peaked cap and jodhpurs, and highly polished leather gaiters. Brabinger had seen the transition from pony trap to motor car, and though he accepted that one was merely the other without the horse, he failed to see why chauffeurs in this day and age continued to dress for the saddle. Particularly when in his case they weren't allowed on the road.

But this was not among his thoughts as he went upstairs and knocked on Audrey's bedroom door.

'It's nearly twelve, madam,' he said. 'Your cases?'

'Yes, I'll bring them down now.'

Audrey had changed. In a cape over a tweed coat and skirt, and suede shoes, she was dressed for travelling. She was sitting on the bare bedstead, looking round a gutted room.

The numbness was returning. She surprised herself by being unable to summon up feelings about the room or leaving it, as well she might since a room without her things in it, her curtains, her pictures and — dare she say it — her woolly panda, was just so much empty space.

She picked up the cases and went downstairs, putting them down in the hall on the way to the drawing room.

The drawing room was empty. Her footsteps echoed, and a floorboard creaked, a sound which rose unimpeded and bounced back off the ornamental ceiling so that it sounded like one of the cherubs sniggering. It was eerie. And full of memories. She stood in silence until her reverie was interrupted.

'Ah, there you are,' said a raucous voice behind her. She wished this, too, had been a figment of past memory, but alas it was all too much in the present and the flesh. It was the rector, for ever the proverbial bad penny.

'It's twelve, you know.'

'I know,' said Audrey calmly.

79

'So you're going, are you?'

'No, I'm queueing for the sales.'

'It's not too late to change your mind, you know.'

'I have made my decision. I'm leaving, and I am absolutely sick of everybody trying to persuade me otherwise. Trust them to get you to make the final appeal, though I can't think of any religious grounds to make me change my mind.'

The rector sighed.

'You won't lose face, you know. Anyway, as I never cease to remind you in church — blessed are the meek, for they shall inherit the earth.'

'And as I never cease to remind you, rector — the meek don't *want* it.'

'I see,' said the rector. 'Well, if I can be of any spiritual comfort at this time of parting ...'

'I don't think last rites will be necessary. The Indians have a saying, "Pray to God, but row away from the rocks". You pray. I'll row.'

'As you wish.'

Brabinger appeared at the door — holding a dog basket with Bertie sitting in it imperially.

'The car is waiting, madam, and the staff are assembled.'

They went into the hall, where the Midionites were hovering uneasily. Mrs Beacham the cook, Millie the maid, Linda Cartwright the groom's help, Ned, the mechanic, the gamekeeper, gardeners, all the tractor drivers, and a host of well-wishers — too many to say much else than a collective 'good-bye'.

This was the test. Would she show signs of weakness, would her eyes glisten? Just because Marjory was already weeping was no reason why she should. All eyes were on her. At the end of a line of faces was the open door, and beyond that, the Rolls where Brabinger had taken up his position. So had the police escort, Constable Peaslake, who, remembering '47, was in position ready to pounce on

Brabinger the minute he hit the public highway. It was to be the longest few yards of her life.

'Good-bye, Mrs Beacham. I'll miss your dumplings.'

'Thank you, m'm. We'll miss you, m'm.'

'Good-bye, Millie,' she said, coming to the young house-help. 'If there's one thing I've taught you since you've been here, let it be that you don't open tins of instant coffee with the best silver.'

'Good-bye, Ned — good luck with your cucumbers at the show. Good-bye, Linda — say good-bye to the horses for me.'

She came to Marjory, who was sobbing into her handkerchief.

'I do hope you'll be happy in the new house.'

'It's all right, Marjory. It's not as if I'm leaving the country.' She passed down the line, bestowing pleasantries, until she came to the rector, for whom she was hard put to think of one. She shook his hand.

'By the way, rector — the church clock is striking thirteen again.' Autocratic to the last.

She took a last look round her, a visual sweep which took in DeVere and his mother who were appearing in the gallery above her. Audrey looked up at them, and decided this was the moment to go.

She wanted to run out of the door, but dignity restrained her. She went through the door slowly, and out into the forecourt, the Midionites spilling out behind her and thronging the car. Brabinger ushered her into the driver's seat, then put on his thick spectacles and skirting the back of the car got in the passenger seat by her side with Bertie. DeVere and his mother were fighting their way through the crowd to add their voices to the chorus of good wishes.

'Good-bye, and thank you all,' said Audrey, with unsuitable buoyancy — almost triumph. She caught sight of DeVere emerging from the front of the group.

'Audrey,' he was calling.

She turned without a flicker of emotion.

'If any letters come for me, *you* pay them.'

Then the engine burst into life, wheel spun on gravel, and they were off.

The group stood transfixed and, for a few seconds, watched the Rolls glide up the drive in awed silence.

They saw the brakelights flash and the car slowed down. Those who were already turning back into the house stopped. Had she forgotten something? Now, instead of seeing the car disappear over the top of the valley ridge into oblivion, they saw the Rolls turn into the driveway of the old lodge. What was going on? The rector noticed it first. The 'For Sale' notice which for months had stood outside the old lodge had been taken down. Through the trees the send-off party could see the car drive up to the front door. Audrey got out of the Rolls and went up to the porch and waved back at the send-off party. Even at that distance, they could see a broad, triumphant smile on her face. Then she walked into the house for all the world — yes — as if she owned the place. Audrey fforbes-Hamilton, late of Grantleigh Manor, had forsaken all that she held dear and broken all ties, but only to start a new life — a mere two hundred yards away.

4

According to Anderson & ffitch, which first brought Richard DeVere to Grantleigh, the old lodge was a 'tasteful conversion'. If this was taken to mean that it had been converted from something tasteful into something tasteless, it would be near the mark. Successive owners had modernized it, obliterating all its old features and its interior had degenerated into the bland style of a period which Audrey dubbed 'mock Recency'.

Only the hall had retained its original style and dimensions, but it led off into silly little rooms which would have been better placed on a housing estate in Basildon.

Futhermore, a previous owner appeared to have a grudge against heat. First, he'd removed any doors which might have kept it in, in favour of allowing free passage from room to room without let or hindrance, and all the fireplaces were horrid little tiled objects much too small to heat the enlarged rooms.

But, of course, it was its position which Audrey found so irresistably attractive, offering as it did an unobstructed view of the manor, its comings and goings, and even much of what went on behind that stately façade. She was now seeing builders' vans parked outside and workmen coming and going, and was consumed with curiosity as to what DeVere was doing.

Since she had hardly left the manor in body, she certainly hadn't left it in spirit, but was clinging to it like a phantom limb after an amputation.

The triumph of her little deception with DeVere, coupled with her establishing a bridgehead from which she could keep an eye on him, sweetened the pill of her otherwise disastrous change of circumstances. She was also strengthened by her unerring sense of destiny and confidence that one day the worm would turn and she would be back in the manor.

All this apart, it was problems all the way. But they tended not to be the ones she anticipated. She expected, for instance, to find living in a confined space unutterably claustrophobic. But even while her new living quarters were not decorated, carpeted and curtained, and while builders occupied every available space, knocking down walls and tearing up floorboards, she found it bearable. She even found the actual experience of sharing a bathroom much less abhorrent than the theory, except that Brabinger would keep using her Ladyshave.

And then, of course, she gradually became aware of new privations which she had not anticipated at all.

For instance, she could not have foreseen that one of the most painful experiences of the move was to be the trivial act of crossing out 'Grantleigh Manor' from her printed writing paper, when informing her friends of her change of address. This led her to another agony, that of asking herself who her friends were, a question which had never arisen before since in her former position her circle had been rigidly prescribed. This in turn led her to realize that if her friends just included those who had rallied to her in her hour of need, then she only had a handful. And if her friends were those people who were now inviting her to dinner parties and the like to ease the misery of her husbandless state, then she had none. The sudden realization that there were absolutely no invitations on the horrid little mantelpiece was traumatic.

'The mantelpiece at the manor positively bristled with

stiffies,' she recalled indignantly to Marjory, who was always round at the old lodge helping her settle in.

'Dinner parties, balls, coming-outs, society weddings, Henley, Ascot, Goodwood, Glyndebourne,' she listed nostalgically, 'to think that I won't be going to Glyndebourne this year, and I used to so enjoy it — apart from having to sit through all those interminable operas. Fair-weather friends all of them — suddenly I'm a social pariah. No invitations — not so much as a Tupperware party in the village.'

Marjory tried to comfort her, and pointed to two conspicuous cards on the mantelpiece.

'What are those two?'

'Oh, real social highlights, these.' She picked them up and read them. 'An invitation to patronize Fonacar Cabs and to have my drain problem solved.' She had written 'refused' on both.

Audrey went to her handbag in search of further evidence. She looked at her diary and flicked its pages under Marjory's nose. The front was crammed full of tiny writing and the later pages were blank.

'We were really in demand till Marton died — now look what I've got to look forward to.' She consulted the diary. 'The Muslim New Year, and High Tide in Aberystwyth. And nothing to wear for either.'

Since their last encounter the day she left the manor, Audrey's attitude to DeVere had mellowed. Part of this was due to her pride that she left the manor nobly, rather than fall in with his plans. She had delivered one body blow and was now entrenched in a position from which more could follow if he stepped out of line. Furthermore, she was in a position to formulate and execute her own manoeuvres which would lead her back to her first love — the manor. That DeVere was quite beyond the pale was without question, but that was not to say that he couldn't eventually be moulded into a suitable match for her. In this enterprise she must be circumspect and cautious, lest she rule herself out as a suitable partner for him. Hence, at this stage in the relationship, she was content to bide her time, seeming neither overanxious to ingratiate herself nor to appear to threaten him. But this was easier said than done. Eager though she was that relations should be cordial, this did not give DeVere the right to trample all over her.

He was doing this unwittingly, but with Audrey being constantly reminded of her humbled position in the neighbourhood *vis-à-vis* his exalted status, he might as well have been trampling in public and in spikes. It was at their first meeting after the move that things came to a head. The battleground was at the village post office.

'Really, the price of ninepenny stamps these days,' Audrey complained as the old harridan pushed the perforated sheet under the grill.

'Always been 9p, dear,' said Mrs Patterson, the postmistress.

'Not nine p. Nine *pence*. A *pea* is a little green vegetable which grow in a pod. Now, could I pay for my papers, Mrs P?'

'Have to take for them separate, dear.'

It was one of the facts of life in Mrs Patterson's shop that everything had to be 'took for separate' — the post office, the groceries section, the off-license, the newspapers department, and she had tills dotted all over the shop, each guarded by a spiteful-looking cat.

Mrs Patterson was thumbing through her newspaper account book.

'Now, it's Mrs fforbes-Hamilton, isn't it?' she said as if she needed reminding, 'of Grantleigh Manor...?

'No, it's the old lodge now.' The admission did not come easily.

'Ah, yes — how is it there?'

'Small.'

'And how's Mr DeVere doing up at your old place — they

86

say he's knocking hell out of the old manor.'

'I wouldn't know.'

'Nice man — if you see him, would you tell him his cigars are in and so is his *Horse and Hound*.'

The intimation that DeVere might be a hunting man came as a surprise. She wondered about it as Mrs Patterson took her money for the papers, and then totted up her groceries and 'took separate' for them.

'That'll be £5.16,' she said, bringing a little notice down from the top of some sweet jars. It said, 'Please do not ask for credit — a refusal might offend.' Audrey pretended she hadn't seen it, and paid.

'Was there anything else, dear?' This was only the third time she had been called 'dear' in the last twenty-five years. All of them had been in the last minute or so, a symptom that her reduction in circumstances was being noted.

Audrey bore the slight with fortitude. There was one other thing to buy, and she could see it in the cold display cabinet.

'Could I have that breaded ham, please?'

'I'm sorry, dear,' said Mrs Patterson. 'I'm keeping it back for old Mrs Cartwright. Her Linda's picking it up sometime.'

Audrey boiled. Linda was supposed to be working for her.

'Mrs Cartwright? The herdman's wife? Since when has she taken preference over....'

No, no, Audrey was telling herself. Control. Dignity. Don't give them the satisfaction of seeing that it hurts.

Her sentence was cut short anyway by the ringing of the shop bell. The door opened and DeVere was standing beside Audrey at the counter.

'Morning, Audrey.'

'Good morning, Mr DeVere.'

'Nice weather for the time of day, as the old country saying goes.'

Audrey ignored it and said coldly, 'Your cigars are in.'

'Ah — just passing by on the off chance.'

'And your *Horse and Hound*,' said Mrs Patterson handing the items over the counter.

DeVere fumbled in his pocket and jangled his money, but Mrs Patterson removed the 'No Credit' notice from him, as deftly as she had displayed it for Audrey. DeVere put his money away.

'Thank you.'

'Was there anything else?'

'Yes. I wonder if you have such a thing as ...'

The shop bell rang, and he turned round.

Audrey was gone.

She had stepped out into Main Street, that is to say, the only street in Grantleigh village. Parked ostentatiously, or so she thought, was DeVere's Rolls. She looked at it as if contemplating an act of vandalism, but was sufficiently self-aware to realize that her own Rolls parked round the corner by the horse-trough was having much the same effect. She had just come face to face with DeVere for the first time since her departure from the manor, and she had plenty to say to him and he had plenty of information she would like from him.

She hovered outside the shop, and read the display of cards in the window advertising for home-helps to do light cleaning. There seemed to be an extraordinary number of dirty lights in the neighbourhood. She smiled at Mrs Hodge's advertisement — 'Let me do your dressmaking and have a perfect fit.' There was a Grand Carpet Sale in Marlbury, with the inducement to 'get felt free', which sounded interesting. But it was another advertisement which caught her eye:

FREE SECRETARIAL COURSE
Offered to any girl in
vicinity likely to be available

> *for temporary work with local*
> *company.*
> *Apply: Richard DeVere*
> *Cavendish Foods*
> *Grantleigh Manor*

She then walked a little way up the road and back again past the shop door in the hope of their paths crossing. DeVere did not emerge. She tried the same dummy run a second time, and DeVere did not rise to the bait. She had just turned back for a third approach when the shop bell rang and DeVere stepped out into the street and hailed her. Audrey spun round.

'Are you going home, Audrey?'

'Yes.'

DeVere pointed the other way down the road.

'It's that way.'

Audrey did not react to this, because she noticed that DeVere was holding a breaded ham. He noticed her looking at it.

'Now who would have thought you could get a breaded ham just like that' — he flicked his fingers — 'in the middle of the country?'

'Indeed,' agreed Audrey. 'These days, all the best pigs seem to be moving into the towns.'

With that, she set off in the direction DeVere had indicated.

'Are you walking?' he shouted after her, when she was a little way down the road.

Audrey looked at her feet in disbelief.

'So I am. I wondered what it was I was doing.'

'Can I offer you a lift?'

'Oh — if it's not taking you out of your way.'

'I live on the estate, don't I?'

'Oh, I know, Mr DeVere. Believe me, I know.'

She was coming back. DeVere, the perfect gentleman,

opened the passenger door without the spur of it being either a new car or a new wife, and ushered her in, a chivalrous act which he then ruined by tossing the breaded ham after her, so that it landed on her lap, shedding a crumb or two. Getting into the driver's seat, he tossed *Horse and Hound* into the back and lit a cigar. He started the engine and the car moved off.

'Home, James, and don't spare the horses,' he yelled, and then, in a voice he thought passed for a west country accent, 'giddy-up'. 'Isn't that what you say?'

'No.'

'Mush.'

'Not to horses.'

'I'm sorry, I forgot I was talking to the Anna Sewell of the Avon Valley.'

Audrey was not amused, but sat there ram-rod stiff, staring ahead of her. She did not know that round the corner by the horse-trough, PC Peaslake had drawn up on his motorcycle, and was slapping a parking ticket on her windscreen. She wondered whether she had made the right decision in choosing this moment to make her first move with DeVere. Now she was in his car, she was no longer on neutral territory.

'The French have a word for it, you know,' said DeVere, after an uneasy silence.

'What?'

'I don't know, but the English word doesn't seem to be getting through. Better out than in, you know.'

Audrey steeled herself for a showdown.

'I don't know where to start,' she said. 'It's one thing after another, isn't it?'

She took a deep breath.

'First you take my ... then you take my ... and then,' words were failing her fast. In an effort to come up with some kind of inventory of the privation she had suffered at his hands, the details had gone completely out of her head.

The only one that she could be sure of was a breaded ham which she clutched like a bludgeon, but what really hurt was that she had been called 'dear' by Mrs Patterson.

'I'm sorry,' said DeVere.

'If you were sorry,' she said, 'you would ...' she had seen that if he was sorry, there was nothing he could do about it. She changed the subject.

'I must say I'm surprised to see you're doing your own shopping.'

'I wouldn't normally, but I've given my girl the morning off to go to a typing course.'

'Yes, I saw your notice.'

'I'm bringing prosperity to an under-privileged area,' he boasted. 'I could do a lot for this valley.'

'I'm sure you could,' said Audrey acidly.

'I beg your pardon?'

'Nothing.'

DeVere continued his self-advertisement.

'I'm supporting local industry,' he said, puffing cigar smoke, 'like I get my cigars through Mrs Patterson.'

That sounded like hard work. Audrey fanned the fumey air vigorously.

'Who is the girl who does your shopping, by the way?'

'The Cartwright girl.'

'Linda?'

'That's right. The horsey one.'

'I didn't realize she worked for you.'

'Oh, yes. Only today she's on a secretarial course. Come to think of it, I'm surprised to see you doing your own shopping. Who usually does yours?'

'Linda Cartwright.'

This was a bombshell. Linda Cartwright was also Audrey's employee. She adopted a defeatist tone.

'So now you take my domestic. Well, it was only to be expected.'

DeVere looked to the heavens through his automatic

sun-roof.

'Oh, my God, so that's it. *Mea culpa*. I'm sorry, Audrey. I had no idea. She didn't say.'

'No, she wouldn't. I expect you're paying her far more than I could. You'll have my entire staff before you're through.'

'That's the last thing I want.'

'And it's the last thing I've got.'

DeVere felt himself to be the victim of a malevolent imagination, and he was going to have to get used to it.

'I wouldn't have done that if I'd known. You've got me all wrong. You don't think too much of me, do you?'

'Whatever do you mean? There isn't an uncharitable bone in my body.'

'That leaves the nervous system and the bloodstream. All right, if I've got to prove that I'm no ogre, what would you say to Linda Cartwright being on my payroll to work for you?'

Audrey was tempted by this gesture, but to accept would not be true to the part she was playing. 'No charity' was becoming her motto.

'And then spend the rest of my life making it up to you? No, no, not me. Anyway, that's not my main concern.'

'You mean there's more?'sighed DeVere wearily. 'All right, wheel out the big guns. What is it?'

Audrey was beginning to get the feel of this encounter and a list of grievances was being drawn up in her subconscious which now appeared before her like an agenda.

'Mrs Patterson says you've been, as she puts it, "knocking hell out of the manor". I want to know what you're doing.'

'Nothing drastic. I'm leaving the foundations.'

'Why? They're the worst bits.'

DeVere felt her animosity boring into him. His business experience was that the best way to deal with hostility is to make light of it, and toy with those who harbour it, as cat with mouse.

'Yes, I'm knocking all the walls down. It's a Japanese idea — to make the interior design blend with the outside landscape.'

He laughed as he saw that Audrey appeared to be believing him, and said more seriously. 'No, I'm just doing some things in your husband's study to make it my personal office. We call it functionalizing.'

'That's a big word.'

'It's a big room. Personally, I prefer the more genteel description.'

'Which is?'

'Knocking hell out of it.'

Audrey tightened her grip on the breaded ham.

DeVere was bashing on gaily. 'You'd be surprised how well my computer console blends with the fruitwood panelling in the ballroom.' He looked at her for a reaction, and it was clear from the optic daggers that she returned that he had overstepped the mark.

'I'm sorry, Audrey,' he said in a conciliatory tone, 'it's just that you rise to it, like a trout to a fat fly. Pardon my choice of words. How's your house, by the way?'

'Small.'

She was clearly dissatisfied with the place — a fact which DeVere seized on to atone for his lack of good grace. He might even score more in the likeability rating by pursuing this line of enquiry.

'If there are any alterations you'd like to make, my builders could always be at your disposal, and at my expense, of course, but that goes without saying.'

'That's very kind, but no thank you.'

'Is there anything else you want?'

'A horse!' Audrey was staring wide-eyed at the road ahead of her. 'Slow down for heaven's sake.'

DeVere was driving faster than was customary along

these narrow country lanes, and, turning a corner, Audrey had been the first to see a horse and rider coming towards them on the narrow verge.

'Slower, slower,' Audrey was begging. 'Snail's pace.'

DeVere did as he was asked, but without seeing why.

'We're in the country now,' said Audrey as they crept past the horse to the acknowledgement of the amply busted adolescent in its saddle.

'We don't race around the lanes on cubbing days,' she admonished. 'Nor do we brush past horses at 90 m.p.h. honking our Colonel Bogey hooters.'

DeVere stood corrected and flicked his fingers in self-deprecation.

'Tch. Of course not,' he said. 'No, that's cows, isn't it?'

They were now past the horse and moving up to the car's former speed.

'Who did you say did your shopping for you?' DeVere asked.

'Linda Cartwright. And who did you say you were paying a fortune to go on a secretarial course today?'

'Linda Cartwright. And who was that on the horse?'

'Linda Cartwright,' they chorused in unison.

Audrey smiled.

'And do you know something? She's on the way to the shop for her mother. To pick up a breaded ham.' She laughed and loosened her grip on the Cartwright Sunday lunch.

For the rest of the journey, they found themselves in complete agreement. This concensus of opinion was that Constable Peaslake was unnecessarily bombastic. The subject arose when a police motorcycle appeared from nowhere as they sped along the main road and hee-hawed them to a halt.

Book in hand, the constable was just giving DeVere the 'you were doing eighty-five — what is it? — is the lady having a baby or something?' recital, when Audrey leant over to make sure Peaslake realized who the lady was.

'Perhaps you haven't met Mr DeVere, constable,' she said, as if Peaslake was on a social call. 'Your father's new employer.'

The notebook went away.

'Just checking you haven't seen any escaped convicts,' the constable improvised rather obviously.

Audrey knew the nearest prison was fifty miles away.

'Just so that if you see anyone hitching, you'll know.'

'Yes,' said Audrey, 'we'll know if they're going this way, they'll be on their way back to prison.

Peaslake stomped back to his chattering motorcycle and rode off.

Soon they were back in the forecourt of the old lodge.

'Most girls I give lifts to like to play with the gadgets,' said DeVere as he dropped Audrey off.

'Most girls haven't been in Rolls-Royces before.'

'Don't you even want to use the car phone?'

'No, thanks — I'll write. Good-bye, Mr DeVere.'

DeVere drove off to the manor, leaving Audrey standing in the forecourt. She waved a breaded ham at him.

'Yours, I think,' she called after him, faintly lest she be heard. She put it into her basket and walked in the front door.

The hall was in chaos. Floorboards were up and wires were trailing about all over the place, and the house had that dusty atmosphere which denotes the transformation of masonry from wall to rubble. She thought the builders had finished. She heard a thump upstairs.

'Brabinger,' she shouted up the stairwell. Stairwell? Hah!! In this little hutch? Brabinger appeared halfway up the stairs. He wore his leather apron and waistcoat, and it appeared that his sleevegarters had not kept his cuffs, which were wet, out of mischief. He was holding a dead pigeon.

'What on earth are you doing?' demanded Audrey.

95

'I'm doing the rewiring, madam.'

'I see. With a pigeon?'

'No, no, madam. I found this floating in the water tank.'

'I was going to say! I've heard of detecting gas leaks with canaries, but I didn't realize electricity had any equivalent.'

The implications of Brabinger's find took a little time to percolate.

'In the water tank?' she screamed. 'Oh, how awful!'

'It's all right. It's dead.'

'Yes, but to think that my bath water comes out of that tap. I've washed in it — I've drunk it.' She clutched her throat and choked dramatically.

'Ye Gods, I've arranged flowers in that water.'

'I'm sure they'll grow the better for it.'

'*And* that's the water I took up to the church for the Cartwright christening. What a way to welcome a newborn into the bosom of the church. To dunk his head into the entrails of a dead pigeon.'

'If the baby grows into a seven-footer, you'll know what's done it, madam,' he laughed, adding as an afterthought, 'if I may be allowed to say so.'

'No, you may not — may I remind you that you are still "downstairs" in spite of the shortage of stairs. I feel quite ill. Anyway, what were you doing in the loft — the wiring's all done.'

'It's *my* system, madam.'

'What system?'

'I thought you'd ask. If you'd care to follow me, I'll show you.'

He led her into the kitchen and pointed proudly above the door, where there was now a bell-box where none had been before. Encased in the mahogany frame behind the glass were twenty little portholes marked 'Front Door', 'Back Door', 'Drawing Room', 'Library', 'Morning Room' and 'Bedroom — one to fifteen' and so on, each backed by its little red disc just waiting to wag when service was summoned to any of the rooms.

'Well, I never,' exulted Audrey, putting her shopping down on the table. 'Brabinger — you are ingenious. That's assuming it works.'

'Oh, it does, madam, it does. *Regardez.*'

He disappeared into the hall and a few seconds later the bell-box burst into life. The little red disc behind 'Conservatory' oscillated vigorously back and forth.

'There, madam,' said Brabinger returning, 'the front door.'

'Very good. I don't like to criticize, but the bell-box said "Conservatory".'

'You always were a perfectionist, madam. A small matter. I just have to do a bit of fiddling in the junction box to connect the right wire to the conservatory.'

'But Brabinger, we haven't *got* a conservatory.'

'Ah,' said Brabinger. 'Details, details. Soon we'll have a bell-push in every room — the sitting-room, the dining room, all the bedrooms, the bathroom.'

'Why should I want to summon you to the bathroom? Besides, in a house this size, I can always shout.'

'Well, the loft then, if ever you make it into another room.'

'Oh, marvellous — so that drowning pigeons can summon help.'

'I have only to put the bell mounting in the drawing room, and the job will be done.'

Audrey was very impressed, and felt she was pouring scorn on it.

'Sweet of you to think of it, Brabinger. Congratulations.' She looked at the pigeon. 'Now, do get rid of that thing.'

They were standing face to face when a bell rang. Brabinger was looking beyond Audrey at the back door, where Marjory had appeared, and Audrey was looking at the bell-box.

'Your services appear to be required.'

97

'It's Miss Frobisher, madam.'

'Then what is she doing in "Bedroom Three"?'

She turned and saw Marjory. Brabinger had already opened the door, and stood with the dead pigeon still dangling from his fingers.

'Morning, Brabinger,' chirped Marjory. 'Yuh!' She recoiled from the pigeon. 'What's that pigeon doing?'

'Not a great deal,' said Audrey.

'Where's it come from?'

Brabinger began, 'I found it in the ...' but was soon cut off.

'Brabinger shot it, didn't you, Brabinger?'Audrey interjected.

'But it's drenched,' Marjory objected.

'With a water pistol.'

'Oh, good shot, Brabinger.'

That was all right, then. Audrey swooped on Marjory and engulfed her with pleasantries.

'Oh, Marjory, I'm so thankful to see you. There's something I want to tell you.'

She put her arm around her and bulldozed her through the hall into the drawing room, with a passing instruction to Brabinger-cum-pigeon.

'Oh, when you've got rid of that object, there's something you and Ned can do for me. I forgot something when I drove back from the village.'

'What would that be, madam?'

'The car,' replied Audrey, tossing him the keys.

The drawing room was still in a state of some disarray though it looked considerably more lived in than it had done for weeks. The carpet was down, the furniture was installed. The curtains were not up, though they lay ready, draped over the back of the armchair. It lacked refinements, the homely and personal touches provided by

98

ornaments and pictures. These were still in tea chests in the grate.

'Oh, this room is going to be lovely,' said Marjory.

'Yes, but it will never be Versailles — not with that horrid little fireplace. Would you give me a hand with these?'

They heaved a tea chest into the middle of the room and began to unpack it. Marjory was extracting a marble table lamp complete with shade.

'Like a lucky dip, this — only without the sawdust. Do be careful with that.'

'Any breakages during the move?'

'Only one of those lion's-paw table legs. Nasty chip.'

'Oh, dear, those tables are quite rare.'

'This one is now — can't be many tables with three lion's-paws and one pig's trotter.'

She was extracting a fox's brush mounted on a wooden shield. She grimaced at it.

'No,' she judged, 'I don't think I want hunting trophies all around me. A bit tasteless — perhaps you'd like it — it's more your sort of thing.'

She stopped to watch Marjory putting the lamp on an occasional table.

'Lampshade seams should point *into* the wall, Marjory, and *away* from the door where it can't be seen.' Marjory turned it round.

A horse's hoof, mounted on an inscribed silver plinth, was emerging from its wrapping.

'Ah, that is more like it,' said Audrey as she read the inscription. 'Petronella — one of grandfather's best horses — do you realize that this hoof won the St Leger in 1912?'

'On its own?' gasped Marjory.

'Attached to the horse,' she said with a long-suffering sigh. 'What a way to end up — full of paper clips.' She flipped up the silver lid and paper clips spilled out on to the table.

'Oh, yes, we used to have a little joke with this when Marton and I were children. Watch this, Marjory.'

She picked out a paper clip and held it up in one hand. 'Clip,' she said, then she raised the hoof in the other. 'Clop.' Then she banged them down on the table alternately. 'Clip, clop, clip, clop, clip,' she chanted in the rhythm of horses' hooves breaking from trot to canter. She was laughing but gave up when she realized that Marjory hadn't understood the joke.

'We used to play that for hours when we were children.' She thought for a moment and her smile faded. 'What a tedious childhood we must have had.'

'Ah, I see,' said Marjory, triumphantly and laughed.

'Good.'

'Well, of *course* it was attached to the horse.'

Audrey wondered about Marjory sometimes. She gave Marjory the hoof to put on the mantelpiece.

'The rest of her was probably made into glue,' said Audrey sadly.

'It comes to us all.'

'She was the best runner the family ever had. Even better than Marquis, my favourite.'

'What was he best at? Have you got any momentoes of him?'

'He was a stud horse.'

'No — well, I don't suppose you want one of *those* on your mantelpiece!'

'Don't be vulgar, Marjory.'

Marjory was trying to put the hoof on the mantelpiece which, after several falls into the grate, she accepted to be too wide for the narrow ledge, and put it on the windowsill.

'Did you want to see me about something?'

'Did I? Oh, yes.' She didn't know where to begin, but launched into her grievances obliquely.

'I try — I try — now, don't I try, Marjory?'

'It's Mr DeVere, isn't it?'

'Yes — answer me this, Marjory. I don't mind coming to live here — no, really I don't, even if it does add another line to my address, a sure sign that one is on one's way down. No, I can get used to this little shed and having to turn a corner every two feet and treading in the dog's bowl every five minutes. That I can get used to. But am I very silly if I resent DeVere running off with my domestics and joking about it, about him getting preferential treatment at the shop, where I now get called "dear" not to mention the breaded ham. I mean, the whole fabric of society is becoming irreparably unstitched.'

The tantrum had burnt itself out.

'What was the question again?'

'I've forgotten.'

'As I see it, you just have to steel yourself to a more modest lifestyle.'

'That's what I thought you'd say,' she sighed. 'Oh, well, I suppose I can learn to wear curlers in the Washeteria.'

'You don't have to go mad.'

'I think I am going mad sometimes. Driven to it, mind. By him.' She pointed the accusing finger towards the manor. 'If I'm going to get back to the manor, he holds the key. This is between you and me, Marjory. I want to get on with him. I want to. But I can't have any sort of association with a man who I bend over backwards to accommodate and then tries to patronize me with offers of help, money, builders — and typing lessons.'

'Typing lessons?'

'The latest — paying girls for his own use. Typing, that is. He calls it bringing prosperity to the valley.'

'I think you should accept his offers,' said Marjory.

'No. Not while there's nothing I can do for him. If only there was.'

'There are plenty of things you can do for him.'

Audrey's disconsolate mood suddenly changed with the appearance from the tea chest of her favourite picture of herself.

'Ah, look,' she said admiringly. 'There's Marquis and me at Badminton.'

Marjory looked over her shoulder.

'Good heavens, who's that with you?'

'M'm? Who?'

'Isn't that the Queen you're talking to?'

Audrey managed to compound all the elements of surprise.

'So it is — yes, I remember now, she did just happen to be there. She must have just strayed into the picture.'

Marjory hadn't seen through this one, so Audrey could elaborate on the theme.

'It's funny — you don't really think of royalty as being flesh and blood until they're actually standing right in front of you. It was years before I was prepared to accept that they had to eat. I always used to think that old Queen Mary's toque was to keep chocolates in for when she was hungry.'

As she spoke she went towards the fireplace, opening the flap at the back of the picture, thereby making it too wide for the narrow mantelpiece. It fell into the grate.

'Oh, Christopher Colombus!' she growled.

'I don't think it's DeVere at all,' said Marjory. 'I think this little house is getting on your nerves.'

'It is *not*,' Audrey denied. The picture fell in the second attempt to install it in its pride of place.

'I like it.'

The picture fell.

'Yes, I like it.'

It fell again and the glass broke, as if trying to persuade Audrey to change her mind.

'Oh, hell's whiskers!' she screamed, 'I hate it, I hate it, I hate it.'

She collapsed into the Chesterfield, red-faced and gasping for breath. Marjory mercy-dashed to her aid, seizing a carafe of water and glass from the drinks trolley on her way. She quickly dispensed it and handed the glass to Audrey who drank gratefully.

'Thank you, Marjory,' she sighed. Then a thought dawned. 'Oh, my God — pigeons — I'm being poisoned!'

'What? You're delirious.'

'No, it's all right,' said Audrey, suddenly regaining her composure. 'Stay for lunch. I hope you like breaded ham.'

For Brabinger and Ned it was a silent journey back from the village post office. Brabinger sat in the passenger seat of the Rolls while Ned drove. It was only natural that he should resent this arrangement, particularly as Ned did not drive with the respect the car deserved. Particularly as he was driving very fast and erratically along the main road. Particularly as he knew that Ned was trying to frighten him, and to make him utter an oath or two which might have been the first words the two had exchanged for years. What did these two have against each other, to fuel this long-standing feud? Everybody knew. Everybody that is, except the man on the police motorcycle, now overtaking them with his siren blaring. Constable Peaslake waved them down and they pulled in at the side of the road. The police constable dismounted took off his helmet and went to the driver's window.

'Right, Brabinger — I've got you now,' he sneered. His face fell when he saw Ned — his own father — looking at him from the driving seat.

'Oh —' he said, '— just to say I might be late home tonight, dad.' He put his crash helmet on again and went round to Brabinger's side of the car.

'One of these days, Mr Brabinger, one of these days. Remember '47.'

Deprived of a breaded ham, DeVere and Mrs Polouvička made do with a steak lunch from the deep freeze, served by

Linda Cartwright. It was a silent meal in the sense that there was no conversation, though much talking was going on. DeVere did not stop work for lunch but often brought his pocket dictaphone to the table and carried on dictating letters throughout the meal. In retaliation, his mother insisted on having a 'family hour' after lunch, but as this usually meant her sprawling out on the sofa and sleeping, the arrangement suited him as he could carry on working.

But occasionally, the need to talk asserted itself at the lunch table, and today was one of those days.

'This one is to Dr Yoshiaki Tanaguci — House of Perpetual Serenity and Moral Fibre, Dock Street, Osaka,' DeVere was saying into his machine as he rounded the meal off with biscuits and cheese. 'So, if you're ready, Hilda — Dear Dr Yoshiaki, thank you for your confirmation of the Cavendish order of...'

'Bedrich,' said the old lady.

'Sssh, thank you for your confirmation...'

'Bedrich.'

'Oh, do be quiet — not you Hilda,' he said to the machine, 'don't write that. Thank you for your confirmation ...'

'Bedrich.'

'Mother, please.'

'Sorry I spoke. Pardon me for living,' sulked the old lady.

'Excuse me, Hilda,' he said switching his recorder off. 'Now, what is it, Mother?'

'I was just thinking you haven't seen Audrey lately.'

'As a matter of fact, I saw her this morning.'

'I hope you were civil to her.'

'Exemplary — I gave her a lift.'

'She knows a lot of useful people, that girl — be nice to her.'

'You don't have to tell me.'

'Did you ask her to come and advise you about the estate?'

'How could I? She's turned me down once. Anyway, I don't need her help.'

'Bedrich!'

'All right, I could do with it, but if she wants to play hard to get — that's up to her. I'm not going down on my knees.'

'You could ask her to help you in little ways, gently — coax a little, a little service rendered here, a little kindness there, and before you know where she is, she is running the estate without knowing it. Out of little acorns do great oaks grow.'

'No.'

'Why not?'

'Because.'

'Ah — I see — so she frightens you.'

'She does not.'

'She ruffles you.'

'No.'

'But she distracts you a little.'

'Certainly not.'

'They why are you buttering your recording machine?'

'I'm not.'

'Then what's that on there, Bedrich?' she said pointing to the mouthpiece.

'Cheese.'

DeVere threw down his napkin, 'And my name's Richard,' he snapped, and stalked out of the dining room into the privacy of the study. There was no sanctuary there; for a start that was where mother and son returned for the statutory 'family hour'. Secondly, that was where the building work was currently in progress.

The old lady followed him into the room, which was once Marton's old study.

'Did I say something ... Richard?' she said.

DeVere smiled to hear his mother use his adopted name. 'Oh, you're right as usual,' he grumbled.

Thus vindicated, the old lady swaddled herself in a tartan

blanket and spread herself out on the sofa to sleep. DeVere went to his desk and began flicking through the pages of *Horse and Hound*.

He was still reading when two workmen returned from their lunch break. They were halfway through the job of knocking out the old fireplace to make room for a safe. The fireplace was an ugly piece of Victoriana and small, considering the size of the room, but effective enough to throw a generous heat the length and breadth of the grate. It was a simple installation job, but the banging, scraping, prising, crumbling, splintering and the nerve-tingling screech of heavy metal being dragged across stone, amplified by the hollow of the safe, could be heard from the old lodge. But not, it seemed, by old Mrs Polouvička, who could not be wrested from her slumbers, nor her son from *Horse and Hound*. When the workmen finally disappeared through the french window to park the old fireplace on the terrace, admitting a gust of air which dispersed the dust-clouds, the old lady opened an eye.

'Ah — I do so like the country,' she said. 'It's so quiet!'

For Audrey, it was too quiet. If six months previously anybody had suggested that she would be reduced to whiling away her time playing Scrabble with Marjory, she would have laughed in their faces. But that's what she was now doing.

'Well, go on then,' she demanded.

'Oh, is it my turn?' said Marjory, surprised.

She consulted her rack of letters and used the G of Audrey's "gnu" to spell "mantling".

'And what, may I ask, is "mantling"?'

'There is such a word.'

'I've never mantled in my life.'

'And when did you last kill a gnu?'

'It isn't *gnu*, it's *gun*.'

106

'Last week with my little twelve-bore gnu.'

'You're making that word up.'

'I'm not, it's in the dictionary.'

'So it may be, but you've got to know what it is. I know you *dis*mantle things, but that doesn't mean you mantle them again afterwards.'

'It's a noun. Mantling is all the bits round a coat-of-arms.'

'Rubbish. Even I know the technical term for that. It's ...'

She fluttered her hand in the air, in an attempt to draw the trappings of a coat-of-arms. 'You know, the frilly bits,' she said, when the word failed her.

'Mantling,' Marjory insisted.

Brabinger came in with the coffee.

'Oh Brabinger — I wonder if you'd mind getting the dictionary and looking up the word "mantling". You'll find it in the library.'

Brabinger withdrew.

'All right, then. The bookshelf — same difference,' sulked Audrey, when she saw Marjory questioning the word 'library'. 'What's in a word?'

'Twenty-eight points if it's "mantling" — including the triple score.'

'I'm challenging you, Marjory. I think you're taking an unfair advantage of me finishing up with a word known only to you and the Garter-King-At-Arms. Just because your uncle was Rouge Dragon Pursuivant to the late king. You know, I've never played this game before in my life, let alone in the middle of the afternoon when I should be doing something useful.' She clenched her fists.

Brabinger returned with the open dictionary.

'Mantling,' he began. 'Mantling or lambrequin.'

'That's the word I was looking for — lambkin.'

'Lambrequin,' Brabinger continued, 'the drapery round a coat-of-arms.'

Marjory was jubilant.

'Didn't I tell you? I win!' She began to clear the board.

'Just a minute,' protested Audrey staying her hand, consulting the letters on her rack. 'Brabinger, see if there is such a word as "Xcplbdc".'

'Oh, Audrey, why can't you lose gracefully?'

'Because,' replied Audrey, when Brabinger had receded, 'because I refuse to be beaten by somebody who, apart from "mantling", can't put a word of more than three letters together. Look at your brilliant words — cat — dog — pot — nice.'

'That's four letters,' Marjory corrected her.

'Maybe, but it's not a word you should use. It's as bad as saying "pleased to meet you" or "bye-bye".'

A crash from the manor — as of rubble being hurled on to the back of a lorry — interrupted their squabble.

'What was that?' asked Audrey seizing a pair of binoculars from under a cushion on the sofa. They were actually Marton's old military field-glasses with gun-sights on the lenses.

'I can see DeVere in the study,' she said, focusing them on the manor french window. 'Oh, why do all the nastiest maggots choose to live in the rosiest apples?' she wondered. She lowered the binoculars.

'These old bins are very powerful, you know.'

'Must be, if you can see maggots in apples.' Audrey raised the binoculars again — and saw them. Two men staggered through the french window, under the weight of the study fireplace.

'Good God! DeVere is throwing out the fireplace now.'

'Which one?'

'That lovely one from Marton's study.'

'Oh, that old thing,' said Marjory casually.

'What do you mean "that old thing". It's a lovely old and valuable fireplace.'

'Oh, what a fib, Audrey,' came the voice of reason, 'you

108

hate that fireplace.' Indeed she did. It had been installed during the war during the fuel shortage, and though there was wood enough for all on the estate, Marton's father had insisted that the fireplaces should be made smaller *'pour encourager les autres'*. They both knew it.

'You're always saying what a monstrosity it was, and you'd get rid of it someday.'

'That's not the point — it's the principle of the thing. It doesn't give DeVere the right to carve up the place. Anyway, he doesn't know that, he wouldn't know a good fireplace from Adam.'

She looked at her own little grate with its haul of hoof and broken picture. 'Anyway, it's a damned sight better than that little monstrosity over there.'

With that she was in the hall, putting her coat on.

'This wholesale sacrilege must be stopped at once.'

'You mean you just want an excuse to go over and see what he's up to.'

'That's got nothing to do with it.'

The door slammed. The house shook and the bell-box in the kitchen tinkled, and every little red disc busied itself behind its porthole. Poor Brabinger didn't know whether he was coming or going.

Linda Cartwright yawned as she showed Audrey into DeVere's presence in the study.

'Does your boyfriend still insist on your going ferreting on Saturday afternoons, Linda?'

'No, ma'am,'

'There, didn't I say things would be different?'

'Yes, ma'am. We watch football now.'

Audrey changed the subject.

'I hope you enjoyed your typing lesson this morning,' Audrey chaffed her. 'Tiring, was it?'

'Yes, ma'am.'

'I'm not surprised — for a start you were sitting all wrong, and Cavesson nosebands should go *under* the sidestrap not above it, and the bit was far too low...'

DeVere overheard this rebuke.

'Thank you, Linda,' he said by way of terminating it. The girl withdrew.

'I'm sorry, I haven't mentioned this morning to her yet.'

'No,' said Audrey. 'I expect you've been too busy knocking the house about.' She looked around her, with particular attention to where the fireplace had been, and especial revulsion at the safe which had replaced it.

'It's a safe,' confirmed DeVere, without looking up from his *Horse and Hound*.

'Good gracious,' gasped Audrey. 'I see what you mean by bringing wealth to the valley. I suppose this is where you'll be bringing it to?'

He didn't answer, but left her to run a mocking finger over the metalwork.

'This must be a genuine old safe — 1977 Chubb, no less, doubtless the work of the great Otto Chubb of Lausanne, cabinet maker to the gnomes of Zurich.'

'You're losing me.'

'Well, anyway, it's streets better than an old Adam fireplace.'

'I wouldn't say that.'

'Then why have you got rid of it? That was a real antique Adam.'

'Yes, yes — and Bombay Duck quacks,' he jibed with impatience.

'Well, anything can happen in India.'

'It wasn't antique. It's a 1939 piece of kitsch, put in by your father-in-law during the wartime fuel crisis.'

'Oh.' Audrey was humbled. 'Even so, I don't think you should just throw it away. I mean, it has sentimental value.'

'And what do you suggest I do with it? If I may take your second suggestion first.'

110

'That's up to you — but I think you should know that it's worth a scintilla more than the one I've got. I've got a squalid little thing you can't even get a horse's hoof on.'

'I didn't realize you were keeping a horse in your drawing room.'

'I'm sure if you had your way it would only be a matter of time.'

DeVere got up from behind the desk as if aware of her presence for the first time. He came to where Audrey had parked herself on the arm of the sofa. He presented the open *Horse and Hound* to her, so that she had no alternative but to accept it, and asked, 'Which one of those should I buy?'

It was at a page of advertisements for horses for sale.

'Are you buying a horse?'

'I buy this magazine for the tortoises, but they only seem to have horses for sale this week.'

Audrey was mystified. DeVere buying a horse, or making any concession to the fact that he was living in the country was a step in the right direction.

'If you'd like coffee while we're choosing, I'll get Linda to make us one.'

Audrey accepted, since she wanted to see this through, and DeVere went to his bell-push by what used to be the fireplace and rang.

'Mr DeVere, is this *really* true?'

'Yes, I'm getting you a coffee.'

'No, the horse, I mean.'

'Yes, I'm buying a horse — tomorrow, I'm going to the dealers to look over a few, and I'd be very honoured and grateful if you would be so gracious as to advise me.'

It was said with such unexpected sincerity, indeed chivalry, that the wind was quite taken from her sails.

'But why me?' she said, turning on the little-woman humility which is supposed to go down rather well with boorish types.

'Because anything you don't know about horses I gather isn't worth knowing.'

'I flatter myself...'

'You needn't. It's already been done by everybody else. You have a reputation as a horsewoman.'

He rang the bell again impatiently.

Audrey wanted to be sure that this was not a ploy, another attempt to patronize her.

'Am I right in thinking you want *my* help?'

'Yes, and I know I'll spend the rest of my life making it up to you — but what the hell, you only live once.'

'Well, I'm bound to say...'

'If it's something to do with boots and other feet, save it. Will you help me?'

'But why do you need help with a horse at all?'

'I might have to take it on a test drive.'

Audrey laughed, partly at the idea of a test drive, and partly at his playing into her hands. Was he, though?

'But, surely — you can handle that?'

'Audrey,' he said penitently, like a lecher at confession, 'I have never been on a horse in my life.'

'Where have you *been*?'

'And if you want to know, I'm scared stiff of the things.'

Audrey allowed herself one superior, dismissive hoot. 'Hah! Can't have that — fear travels down the reins very fast.'

'I like to be in control — horses aren't like cars.'

'You can't make telephone calls from a horse, that's true,' she said, turning on the charm and good humour, now convinced that this was a genuine petition.

'Tomorrow, you say?'

'I'll pick you up at two o'clock.'

She looked at her diary and flicked through the empty pages.

'Yes, I might be able to squeeze you in. It's Brabinger's day off and I won't have to be at home for him to cook for.'

112

'That's settled then.'

DeVere rang the bell again.

'Where is that girl?' DeVere huffed. 'I'll sack her if it's the last thing I do.'

DeVere's staff problems gave her additional delight. It suddenly occurred to her why the errant Linda had not responded.

'Never mind the coffee,' she said. 'Another time.'

'Two o'clock tomorrow.'

Audrey was just about to go when a mound of tartan rug on the sofa beside her stirred, and the head of Mrs Polouvička appeared.

'Three o'clock,' demanded the head. 'You're not getting out of family hour *that* easily.'

Audrey recoiled from this interjection and looked at DeVere.

'Three,' he said with filial piety. 'Now where is that girl?'

In the kitchen Linda Cartwright was sleeping soundly in a rocking chair. A few inches above her head a number of loose wires dangled which could be traced to a number of holes further up the wall. The holes were placed neatly in an oblong in the centre of a frame of cobwebs and dust — in fact, the sort of place where a bell-box might just once have been.

Audrey was very excited as she hurried back to the old lodge. DeVere was at her mercy and was about to be in her debt. Besides, his mother with one short sharp sentence had exposed a crack in his armour. A mother complex was to her advantage. In fact, she was so excited that she had to check herself as she came to the front door of the old lodge because she had a little unpleasant duty to perform first. She and Brabinger were going to 'have words'.

She walked in and hung her coat up. The hall was still in the chaos which Brabinger's rewiring had occasioned, in

113

fact, if anything it was worse.

'Brabinger!' she shouted.

'Yes, madam,' said a voice behind her.

'I want a word with you about your bell-box system. It didn't occur to me to ask where you got it from, but if you don't want to join the ranks of the unemployed on the estate, and go to typing classes...'

Her words died on her lips as she turned to see Brabinger. He was filthy. His face and head and shirt were black, and he was covered in soot and bits of straw and twigs. He carried a screwdriver and wires trailed from him. Marjory came out of the drawing room after him — she, too, was tarred with the same brush.

'God be merciful,' exclaimed Audrey, agape. 'Whatever is this? The cast of "Ipi Tombi"?'

'You tell her, Brabinger,' said Marjory.

'I'd rather you did, madam.'

Audrey was impatient. 'Well, come along. One of you tell me.'

'It's good news and bad news,' said Marjory.

Brabinger took the plunge. 'I was fitting my bell mounting by the fireplace and doing a bit of drilling when I discovered that the wall was hollow.'

'How?'

'It was just a tap, madam.'

'*How?*' Audrey repeated.

'And the walls came tumbling down,' sang Marjory.

'Leave Joshua out of it, if you don't mind. That's the good news, is it? So let's have the bad.'

Brabinger went on. 'When the whole fireplace had collapsed ...'

Marjory took up the story.

'...we found underneath that horrid little fireplace was a real old hearth — it's a beauty.'

'Good heavens, really?' Audrey said with disbelief, brushing past them and bursting into the drawing room.

Sure enough there was the huge open fireplace — an inglenook of Portland stone set well back into the chimney. At either side were recesses which led into the original baking ovens. There was even a roasting turn-spit, meat hooks and irons.

'Why, it's beautiful,' marvelled Audrey, stepping into it and looking up the chimney. 'I can't imagine why people closed up these old beauties. I suppose it was a matter of fashion as much as anything.'

'A little job for you, Brabinger,' she said as she stepped out of the inglenook. Brabinger took her place, looking up the chimney and prodded at something above him with a screwdriver.

'Yes, we can have it cleaned up in no time, madam.'

With that, a cascade of soot avalanched down the chimney and inches of black snow nestled on his horizontal surfaces, his head and shoulders; some went down his legs both inside and outside his trousers, and buried his feet to the ankles. A nest and a dead crow brought up the rear, or rather brought it down.

Coughing and spluttering, Brabinger bent down to retrieve the missiles.

He stepped out of the chimney holding up the dead crow.

'Oh, good shot, Brabinger,' laughed Marjory. 'He's having quite a good bag today, isn't he?' mocked Audrey. The two women burst into a fit of schoolgirl giggles. Brabinger did not.

That night the fire was ablaze. It was wonderful sight, and Audrey was in a sunny mood, and she luxuriated before it with Bertie on her lap. She had everything to be pleased about — DeVere was about to be beholden to her which would give her an advantage over him. He was, perhaps, not such a hard nut as she had been led to believe.

'Maybe Marjory is quite wrong about him,' she confided

to the dog. 'Can't think why she's so keen to blacken his name.'

She began to count her blessings. For a start, there was Brabinger's bell system. A brand new mounting had been installed by the fire and it had brought back happy memories of the manor.

She got up and rang it, an act which reminded her that she still had Brabinger, that was another thing to be thankful for. Where would she be without him? Although most of her other domestics were now in DeVere's employ, at least there was no fear of losing Brabinger. Not Brabinger. She laughed and tickled Bertie under the chin. Brabinger did not appear. She got up and rang the bell again. Then she adopted a favourite stance of Marton's, with her back to the fire and launched herself into an impression of him while she waited.

'Put another log on the fire, Brabinger,' she said in Marton's monogrammed voice with its double-breasted vowels, bending her knees. 'That'll make him laugh if I do that when he comes in,' she told the dog.

But Brabinger did not come in. She waited a moment before conceding that the mountain would have to go to Mahomet. She opened the door, peered out of it into the hall. It was cold and dark. A light fanned out from under the kitchen door, and the sound which seeped through that narrow strip did more than merely elevate her hackles. It spelt doom.

It was the sound of a typewriter — slow and faltering, but unmistakeably typing — as of one who is learning, but who still has a long way to go.

Audrey bounded across the hall and threw open the door.

Brabinger leapt from his seat, as if to distance himself from the incriminating evidence — the typewriter and paper.

'I forbid it.' Audrey ordered.

'What, madam?' quavered the startled butler.

116

'I forbid you to take Mr DeVere's secretarial course.'

'I had no intention of doing so, madam. I was merely doing some new labels for this.'

He indicated the bell-box which lay in bits the other side of the typewriter. He had taken it down from the wall above the door and dismantled it. Now he was typing the names of the lodge rooms to stick under the portholes.

'I couldn't get the wiring right, madam,' he explained, 'so I'm changing the names of the rooms.'

Audrey sighed a sigh.

'Oh. Thank you, Brabinger — that will be all.'

Brabinger nervously resumed his task.

Audrey put her own log on the fire.

'There's one born every minute, and I've got one coming in five,' said Frank G. Furgusson, into the nearest available ears. They belonged to a horse, so answer was neither required nor expected. The horse in question was a bay gelding, one of several advertised in *Horse and Hound*, as being for sale by Frank G. Furgusson, dealer, of Swanridge Farm.

'Don't worry, Beauty — I'll find you a good home,' he said, patting the equine nose which snorted, belching steam out over the stable door, like a laundry in winter. That the horse did not reply might well have been because Beauty wasn't its name. All horses which were kept in that particular stall for the days and hours prior to sale were called 'Beauty' unless good cause could be found for not.

It already had a perfectly good name but that was not reason enough. All five horses in the stable yard that day found themselves with new names. It was the same thinking which lay behind the name 'Goliath' (for sales purposes only) for any horse over sixteen hands. If, of course, two horses of over sixteen hands were for sale on the same day, he'd have to come up with another name, which he often

117

took from the early morning radio, inspired perhaps by the week's composer, 'Rimsky Korsakov', or a traffic warning, 'North Circular'.

Furgusson heard a car drive into the yard, came away from the stable door, and alerted the stable lad.

'Come on, boy,' he shouted, 'and remember Beauty is at the back of the queue. He's only worth eight hundred. And make sure that other beggar doesn't limp. Let him lean on you a bit.'

The stable lad jumped to it, taking up a position by the first stall, with a swing of uncoordinated hips and buttocks, and the rapid ebb and flow of free-fall bosoms. Incidentally, the stable boy was a girl, and her anatomy seemed to have been built to a sliding scale.

The Rolls drove down the farm track into the stable yard. First impressions of customers were very important to a salesman, and the impact of the appearance of a Rolls, then DeVere emerging from one door, and Audrey from the other, was that here was both money and discernment, not an easy combination to sell to.

'Mr Furgusson?' said DeVere.

'Mr DeVere,' said Furgusson, shaking his hand, and then moving on to Audrey.

'Mrs DeVere.'

Audrey blenched. Mrs DeVere, indeed! Weren't things moving just a bit too fast? Still, one had to admit it was an easy mistake to make. There was no doubt that she and DeVere did *look* like a couple. They blended well, as if over years of married life, bits of each's individuality had worn off, and stuck to the nearest thing, which happened to be the other.

The journey to the stables had been fun, because DeVere had revealed himself to be so remarkably ignorant of things horsey that it put Audrey back where she'd almost forgotten she belonged — in charge.

DeVere had been irritating her by talking about all

118

equestrian activities as if they were no better than tennis or golf, and the mention of the test drive irked her, but otherwise it had been agreeable. He had sworn her to secrecy that he had never 'driven' a horse in his life. They'd agreed that she'd do all the talking.

'After you ... darling,' said DeVere, as they followed the dealer.

'Have I got just the thing for you,' said Furgusson.

'I don't know — we'd hoped you'd know.'

'A hunter, wasn't it? Course it was.'

'We hope it still is.'

He led them to a stable door in the centre line of stalls. He snapped his fingers and the stable lad led out a chestnut ten-year-old, and took off its rug.

'Look at this little miracle of breeding,' marvelled Furgusson. 'Strips well, eh? Course 'e does. Lovely sort of a horse. He's called Plymouth Rock. This was a name he'd heard in an early morning travel talk and once in a lyric of 'Anything goes', which was played in a breakfast request show.

'...which as its name implies...'

'Comes from Plymouth. Is that significant, Audrey?'

Audrey's look held him to the pledge to let her do the talking.

'Intermediate eventer. A snip at five thousand pounds. Perfect conformation — look at the stamp of this horse — has he got a mouth like velvet — course he has.'

He was laying it on.

'He can keep his place in any hunt and still have a leg to spare.'

'Hear that? He carries a spare,' said DeVere, but Audrey wasn't listening. She scrutinized the creature's legs.

DeVere raised his eyebrows and crouched down beside her.

She whispered, 'If he's showing us the top half, the snag will be down below.'

'That's so often the way,' said DeVere of something completely different. 'What are you looking for? A "Made in Hong-Kong" label?'

Audrey found what she was looking for.

'Here it is,' she said, feeling its fetlock. 'Bowed tendon here, Mr Furgusson. Has this horse been fired?' she said accusingly.

'Not that I know. Real genuine animal, this.'

'True. I saw it move,' said DeVere.

'Would you be quiet, Mr DeVere,' she said — then to Furgusson, 'Take him away. The horse, I mean.'

'Lad,' shouted Furgusson, snapping his fingers. The 'lad' led the horse away.

'Sorry, son, don't call us,' DeVere commiserated with the animal.

The 'lad' returned with Fearless — the fourth Fearless of the week — a more slenderly built horse, black, with a blaze on its nose and white socks.

'Three thousand,' said Furgusson, coming to the point. 'Wasn't broken till he was five. I've seen him take a five-foot-six fence out of a trot, haven't you, Fearless? Natural impulsion's a joy to behold. Poetry on legs.'

DeVere liked the look of this horse, but his picture of himself astride it in shining armour evaporated with an emphatic 'no' from Audrey before she had even inspected it.

'What's wrong with it?' said DeVere not concealing his dire disappointment.

'No courage,' said Audrey. 'Shows too much white for a start.'

'And for seconds?'

'The name. Fearless. He's probably only had that name since this morning and he's called that because Furgusson knows he's an absolute coward. It's an old trick. If ever you're offered a horse called "Utter Rubbish", buy it.'

As the horse was led away by the stable lad with her poor

120

conformation of buttock and bosom, Audrey addressed Furgusson.

'I wonder if you have something which might be suitable for someone to learn on?'

The shetland pony which was led out for a breath of fresh air, might have got that breath, but no more before it was back in its stall.

'Who is this for, madam?' asked Furgusson.

DeVere feared exposure, but Audrey acted honorably.

'Is it for yourself, madam?'

'Yes, it is, isn't it ... darling?' said DeVere.

Audrey didn't deny it.

Furgusson was sizing her up.

'Fifteen stone ... in her city suit,' said DeVere.

While Furgusson was briefing the lad, Audrey drew DeVere aside and dressed him down with clenched teeth.

'Will you *please* take this seriously?'

DeVere stood chastened, and actually felt it.

'Good blood horse, this,' said Furgusson as the seventeen-hand 'Goliath' was led out. 'Not going for cob, are you? Of course you're not. I always find a big woman very difficult to mount, don't you, sir?' Furgusson allowed himself a laugh, and looked to DeVere to share it with.

DeVere restrained himself for Audrey's sake.

'Five thousand — a real, good Christian, this — you won't find a better this side of the Severn Estuary — not heavy-weight hunters.'

'No,' said Audrey again to DeVere's chagrin. 'No bone — big body, but the legs aren't strong enough for it — let alone, you.' She corrected herself. 'Me.'

'Could have done with this feller at Cheltenham a couple of years back.'

'I'm sure,' said Audrey, sizing the beast up. 'You'd have got a much better view of the racecourse.'

'But there's a good few seasons left in this horse.'

'I believe you. Pantomine seasons,' said Audrey.

121

DeVere felt like applauding and laughed. Audrey couldn't, but the evident success of this excursion was giving her great pleasure — she took advantage of Furgusson's turned back to thumb her nose at DeVere.

'Is that all you have?'

'There is one, but ... well, you'd be much better off with....'

'Let's see it.'

A solid-looking Irish hunter was led out. It was Beauty.

'Not what I'd call a horse. I mean, not when you compare it with the others.'

He could see Audrey was not going to rule this one out of court.

'With respect, I don't think that horse is really *you*.'

'I'm gratified that you can tell us apart,' she said, stroking the horse.

'Actually, madam,' said Furgusson playing his cards close to the vest, 'he's really my own. You'd be much better off with one of the others.'

'Very smart — yes, I think he'd be just the thing.' Audrey was saying as she looked over the horse. 'Fifteen hands, good athletic build, strong legs, it'll last you for years — no neuroses.'

'I tell you he's my own. He's not for sale. I wouldn't part with him for ...'

'Seven hundred and fifty?' said Audrey casually.

'Sold!'

'I make it I owe you £4250,' said DeVere in the car on the way back to the manor.

Audrey was pleased with her success and was not going to over-react to the compliments — she wanted to store up reserves of kudos while the going was good.

'Oh, don't be silly,' she said, coyly.

'You saved me a lot of money. I mean, the way you

122

spotted that — what was it?'

'Bowed tendon.'

'Very clever. Mind you, I was the clever one. I went to the right person.'

'Well, thank you.'

'How did you do it — how did you *know*? Woman's intuition?'

'Brainpower and experience.'

'Next question. Why did you do it?'

This was below the belt.

'What do you mean. Why?'

The answer was important and he slowed the car down to hear it.

'Why did you get me a good-natured creature that'll last? You could have got me a bad-tempered geriatric with one wooden leg which would have thrown me and bitten my head off on the way down. I wouldn't be any the wiser, at least unless I happen to spot his stitches in the showers one day — you could have done that.'

Audrey fixed him in a searching gaze.

'How do you know I haven't?'

'Trust,' said DeVere. 'We've got to live together, haven't we?'

'That's what I thought, too.'

They were closing in on each other.

'But you did think of it, didn't you?'

'Of course,' said Audrey.

They understood each other. A breakthrough had been made. The sparring was over and their guards fell. They began to laugh.

'Audrey, you are amazing. Am — az — ing!' DeVere yelled to the world at large through the open window. He put his foot down and the car jerked forward to resume its natural speed — breakneck.

'You're wonderful, Audrey — out of this world. Let's go and get a drink somewhere before we go home.'

'That would be lovely.'

'Then perhaps you could look at this leg of mine. There might be a bowed tendon in it for you.'

On the way home they called in at the Harborough Arms, a convivial restaurant with equestrian awnings, and roaring fires where at one time local gentry would take dinner on the staff night off. These days it appeared that the gentry tended to cook for themselves at home and the staff came to what they referred to as 'the Rip-off Arms'. The building was set into the perimeter wall of the Harborough Hall estate, and the alcove allocated to Audrey and DeVere commanded a good view of the hall itself, a gigantic pile sited on a mound surrounded by a deer park.

Anxious not to talk about herself, Audrey was very happy to talk about Harborough and gossip about the Mortlake family. DeVere had heard much of it before from Lady Mortlake herself at the party after Marton's funeral, but was interested to hear the other side of the story.

'Of course there was no doubt whatever that they started the fire which destroyed old Grantleigh,' she told him. 'I mean, the rivalry was getting just silly, and it was the only way they could win. They were both trying to be the first to come up with a sundial with a second hand at the time; that's how silly it was getting.'

They were interrupted by a voice from the other side of their high-backed wooden seat which separated their alcove from the next table.

'Does your horse go to school?' it asked.

The answer was lost in a babble of female conversation.

Audrey went on with her story.

'The present Lord Mortlake is Lord Lieutenant of the county, you know. He's nearly eighty and can't have long to go, but if one will marry a girl forty years one's junior, what does one expect?'

124

De Vere laughed.

'You must meet Celia Mortlake,'

Audrey wondered whether she'd said the right thing. They may be getting on very well *à deux*, but he was hardly yet suitable to introduce to her friends, let alone the titled ones. But it was too late.

'We've already met,' said DeVere. 'At your husband's funeral. She's rather attractive, isn't she?'

'To some tastes, maybe.'

So that was that.

'Mind you, Celia Mortlake had the whole thing worked out. She's an awful snob. There's a lot she can put up with for a title and a stately home, and sleeping with an eighty-year-old is a small price to pay. Particularly when she can still lead her own life. Not that I'd go so far as to say she puts herself about, or anything.'

'Does she?'

'I'm not saying so, no. There is such a thing as loyalty and we're old friends.'

'I thought you were deadly enemies.'

'Heavens, no. One doesn't perpetuate the follies of history. These days even Capulets and Montagues would go to each other's cocktail parties. That old feud between us is long forgotten.'

'Is that so?'

'Well, more or less.'

The afternoon and evening had gone well, but it was too good to last. After the meal, on the way to the coffee lounge, Audrey peered into the adjoining partition. It was a group of ladies having dinner and surrounded with bits of paper and brochures. She recognized them all.

'Those in favour?' said the one with a minute book. 'The pony club gymkhana moves to Harborough this year.'

'Aye,' called the women.

'Carried,' said the chairperson. 'And Heaven help who ever tells Audrey.'

It was dark by the time they got back to the estate. They had chattered amicably about this and that without strain or embarrassment, and indeed Audrey had had more wine than she should. She was a bit giggly when DeVere dropped her off at the old coach house.

'I did enjoy making all those phone calls — thank you for a lovely time … Richard.'

'Thank *you*.'

'Why don't you come in for a nightcap? Brabinger's day off today, so don't expect too much.'

Inside, Bertie was barking and snuffling as if trying to crawl out under the front door.

They went into the house and turned the lights on. The chaos in the hall had not been improved. It also smelt dusty, which reminded Audrey that she had something to show DeVere.

'It's a bit cold, but we'll soon have a fire going.'

'Look in here,' said Audrey, opening the drawing room door and turning the light on.

DeVere held her in the doorway.

'Audrey — I have to tell you this,' he said earnestly. 'There is another reason I took you out today.'

'Naturally. I'm a very attractive woman,' she giggled.

'And a very obstinate one. You have never let me show my esteem for you in my own way. So you've forced me to force you to accept things from me.'

'Things?'

'Yes. I wanted to give you something you said was of great sentimental value — so while we were out today, I took the liberty of sending my builders round to fix it in for you.'

The blood rushed to Audrey's head and then down into her feet.

'Not the …?'

She rushed into the drawing room, where her worst fears were confirmed.

126

Her beautiful inglenook fireplace had been blocked up again, and had been replaced by the Victorian monstrosity which had been in the manor study.

She tried to speak, but words failed her.

'No, no, I don't want thanks,' protested DeVere, 'you've earned it.' He beamed, and plumed himself on the success of his subterfuge.

'Well, what do you think?' he asked.

'I think,' said Audrey coldly, 'I think that I should have bought the horse with the bowed tendons.'

5

Having the inglenook fireplace restored to its original form placed an additional burden upon Audrey's now chronic finances. The resulting upheaval also soured her attitude towards DeVere. She now had the leisure to brood on their relationship, which at one point seemed to be developing so well, and had come to the conclusion that the very name DeVere was synonymous with trouble, and that she would be well advised to steer clear of him. In doing so, she puzzled DeVere, who could not understand why his largesse with the fireplace had fallen on stony ground, and Audrey had done nothing to enlighten him. What's more, she cut him dead every time they met on the estate. This was the price of what in Audrey's book constituted a serious breach of the social code — he had tried to patronize her. For several weeks, during which spring turned to summer, they did not speak.

DeVere, to his surprise, found her snubs hurt. He missed Audrey, and he hated the feeling that the high hopes he'd harboured for a fruitful friendship after their evening together were crumbling about him. He held out for as long as he decently could, without seeming over-anxious to ingratiate himself with her, and then took the initiative to restore relations. He invited her to a cocktail party.

As all hosts and hostesses know, one's social circle is segmented — the people invited into one's house are either friends who's company one enjoys, or they are acquaintances invited out of a sense of duty, those one ought 'to be nice to', those one 'owes', those one feels 'guilty about' — family perhaps. Once you are at a party, it is easy to spot whether this is the 'pleasure' or 'duty' party.

It was a feeling of victory which filled Audrey when she received DeVere's invitation to the manor, but it soon turned to ashes when she arrived to find that she was merely on the 'duty' list, where everybody else's presence merely served to wipe DeVere's social slate clean.

It was a cocktail party and she was just one of sixty or so people. DeVere considered this a stroke of genius, since he could both invite her to the manor, and seem indifferent to her at one and the same time. One way or the other, this was sure to end their war of silence.

She arrived at the party late, a ploy to maximize the impact of her entrance, since this was her comeback on the social circuit. But by that time Mr Widrig, the caterer, had poured so much champagne and forced so many chipolatas down DeVere's guests that they were past caring. She went largely unobserved, except by Mrs Bickerton — the arch-deacon's wife — who swooped upon her with 'Oh, you must hear Gerald's joke — I was just saying that ordinary blankets cost as much as continental quilts — and he said, "Oh, duvet?" ' With which Audrey was alone again.

For a time she just wandered round the room picking up fag ends of conversation.

'I do wish people who run Spanish restaurants would learn that not all English people want Max Bygraves with their Chile Relleno,' said a man with a deep tan. Could it be the same sun which in England turns you red, elsewhere turns you a beautiful bronze, thought Audrey?

'I love Spain,' said a bewhiskered woman, whose plate of food, glass and wrist bag seemed to have toppled her forward at a Pisa-like angle. 'My dear, every taxi, tractor and ox-cart is driven by Anthony Quinn.'

Audrey brushed past several conversations. There was

129

one in which a woman had missed an earthquake 'by a hair'. In another, a man was extolling the Majorcan economy, based, as he claimed, on a mutually satisfying compulsion of the natives to build walls and of tourists to knock them down again.

All the conversations seemed to be about holidays, which reminded Audrey that she had not had a holiday. Not wanting the embarrassment of admitting as much, she set off to forage — via a salver of *cruditées*, and a glass of punch proffered by Mr Widrig — for a conversation on some other topic.

There only appeared to be one. She didn't have to be involved in it, or even near it to know its subject. It was Marjory doing her bird impressions over by the fireplace and for the benefit of DeVere.

'You'll soon get to know the difference,' she was telling him. She did a bird call. 'That's the chaffinch, but the bullfinch is quite different, like this.' She did the same throaty warble. Audrey was interested to hear how DeVere would express interest without lying, but her attention was caught by another conversation.

'Oh, yes, DeVere's loaded all right — don't know where he gets his money from, but they say he sends his laundry to Paris.' Audrey cocked her ear but it was lost in a babble of holiday chatter.

'Poor Reggie was down with Greeks Revenge — I can't think what Moussaka does to the system, but on the waistcoat, it's totally resistant to Dab-it-Off.'

'... and a little place called Port Cervo on the Costa Smerelda, not far from the Aga Khan's villa ...'

"... wonderful hotel, if only they'd change the water in the bedside carafes once in a while ...'

'... simply awful place, darling ... the windows stick and the stamps don't ...'

'... just look at that,' swanked a fat man, lifting his shirt and patting his bronzed midriff proudly. It was Arnold.

'… and all in under a week. Matched it up with the paint chart and it's called "Tuscan". Don't consider the job done until I'm "Deep Caramel"….Oh, hello Audrey.'

At last — somebody had noticed her.

'Arnold,' she acknowledged.

'You know everybody?'

'I think so — good evening.'

'I was just saying how we're off to Spain again next week to finish the tan off,' he said, scooping his stomach back into his trousers in several loads.

'Look at you, Audrey,' said his wife, 'you're looking positively peaky.'

Arnold agreed. 'Whatever colour do you call that? "Magnolia"? "Whitewash"? "Whippet Beige"? How did you get that tan? Sunbathing at night, eh?'

You could see his laugh undulating through his rolls of fat.

'I've been far too busy,' said Audrey icily.

'Still, nice to have you back on the party circuit. I see the Pocklingtons are here, but where are the Wymms-Wellbournes, and I haven't seen the Mortlakes for ages. Perhaps they'll be at your party next week. We're all looking forward to that; not that we're expecting anything as lavish as this — or the Faversham-Ore parties for that matter. Not in your circumstances, anyway.'

This hurt.

'He doesn't have to live on Milk Marketing Board subsidies.'

She walked away.

'What did she mean by that?' said the woman when Audrey had gone.

Audrey gravitated towards the fireplace, but saw Marjory mid-wildlife lecture, and edged away again. It was just as well.

'I love my dickey-birds,' she was saying, 'I'd be completely lost without my feathered friends — and furred ones, too, of course. Especially badgers. There's a badger's sett in the woods at the back of the old lodge.'

'You shouldn't tell me things like that,' yawned DeVere. 'With my reputation, it's the sort of information I'd use to go into business making shaving brushes.'

'Now, who would say things like that?'

'People,' said DeVere. 'Person,' he added, his gaze boring into Audrey's back, as if to burn the label which was hanging conspicuously from her dress.

'Audrey? You know, it would do *her* a lot of good if *she* took more interest in wildlife.'

'I don't think you should expect it,' advised DeVere. 'After all, one doesn't study marine biology when one's drowning.'

Audrey didn't hear this, as she was straining her ears to tune into another exchange of repartee.

'I think DeVere is awfully sweet. They say he's absolutely stinking, and of course he's brightening up the manor no end. One could see it was going to pieces.'

'Ahem,' coughed Audrey.

'Oh, hello, Audrey,' said the woman gushing like an incontinent fire-hydrant. 'I was just saying how the manor has gone to pieces since Mr DeVere's been here.'

Audrey went with the change of tune.

'You'd think he could afford to do something about it, since he's absolutely ... stinking.'

'He's in food, isn't he?'

'So he says,' said Audrey, pointedly.

She moved away from the group, turning so abruptly that the label hanging from the neck of her dress splayed out and made its presence known.

'Allow me,' said a chivalrous man, tearing the label off.

'I say,' said the woman who had read it when Audrey was out of earshot. '"Yves St Laurent". So she can't be *that* hard up.'

Audrey had extricated herself from one conversation

with such force that she lost the power of steering and could not avoid careering headlong into Marjory.

'Oh, Audrey, I haven't seen that dress for ages.'

'Sssh,' whispered Audrey, 'it's new.'

'But I happen to know that you wore it for the Festival of Britain.'

'Yes, but *they* don't,' she sneered with an all-encompassing gesture.

'Are you all right?' asked Marjory with concern. 'You're looking positively peaky.'

'Yes, and if anybody else says that — or that I look as if I need a holiday, I'll scream.'

'No — I was just going to tell you that I've been telling Mr DeVere about the badgers....'

'Sssh,' hissed Audrey, straining her ear to catch another snippet. A brigadier was talking nearby.

'Don't ask, my dear — but they say the food business is a front. I've even heard he's on the run from the police,' he added in confidence. 'Sly devil if you ask me. Sly devil.'

Audrey grinned to herself.

'I'm sorry, I've been ignoring you,' said a voice behind her. It was DeVere.

'Good evening, Mr Devil ...' she said, 'I mean, Mr DeVere.' Yes, it was back to formalities.

'I say, you're looking washed out. You look as if you should take a holiday.'

Audrey stiffened and she wanted to scream, but her good breeding got the better of her.

'Yes, I think I will,' she managed with great self-control.

With that, she turned and melted into the throng — the social battlefield of inane chatter, knee-deep in slopped Pimms, trodden-in potato salad, all canopied in cigarette smoke.

'My dear chap, always get your duty-free on the way *out*,' someone was saying. 'I mean, where can you get a decent Benedictine in France?'

'... and the Faversham-Ores aren't here.'

Audrey was packing. She was frivolously dressed in a summer frock and straw hat. It was the following day, and she was busying herself with what a department store would call 'holiday requisites', and was surrounded by cases, labels, airline bags, and bathing costumes. The only item in the room not wanted on the voyage was Marjory.

'Honestly,' she was saying. 'Fancy putting a label on that old dress.'

'It worked, didn't it?' said Audrey, pretending not to be interested. 'Anyway, according to *The Sunday Times*, it's back in fashion.'

'Surely you can still afford something better?'

'The *Sunday Telegraph*, the *Observer*. I'm sure they're all the same price.'

Brabinger materialized in the doorway in his chauffeur gear.

'Are you ready, madam?'

'Booted and spurred. Those two cases are ready, they can go in the car.'

Marjory, never easily steered off a subject, persisted.

'I think you can go too far for the sake of appearances.'

'Appearances are really all I've got.' said Audrey, remorsefully. 'You've no idea how humiliating it was at the party to hear everybody talking about their holidays. As for the rest, it was just a meeting of the Richard DeVere fan club.'

She resumed her stock-take of holiday requisites.

'Entrovioform, Kwells, Silva-Sun, Dio-Calm ....'

'Even so, there was no need for you to say unkind things about him — by the end of the party everybody was making him out to be some kind of a drug smuggler.'

Audrey beamed.

'I never said anything like that. All I said was that he

wasn't dependent on the Milk Marketing Board.' She turned on Marjory like a startled ferret. 'And I can do without your lectures, thank you very much. I do wish your wildlife rambles wouldn't end up here. You make me feel like an osprey or some endangered species which needs your protection. Why don't you go up to the manor and find out how cuckoos live?' She looked into her suitcase. 'Now will I need a mosquito net?'

Marjory wondered why she might want to catch mosquitos, but asked for an explanation of the remark about cuckoos.

'It *is* cuckoos which throw other birds out of their nests, isn't it?'

'Yes. Oh, I see.'

'Except you won't find him there. He's on holiday from today.'

'Is he?' Marjory exclaimed with some feeling.

'Yes. I thought that would ruffle you. So it's no good thinking you can go and seduce him the moment my back is turned. You don't think I'd go away and let him loose on the estate, do you? This is the only week it's safe for my holiday. Passport, travellers' cheques, secateurs — how did they get in there?'

Audrey shut her case and stood back. 'Well, I think I'm ready.' She zipped up her airline bag and slung it over her shoulder. Brabinger appeared, as a genie to the rubbing of a ring, and followed as Audrey carried the suitcases out into the hall.

'You're still not telling me where you're going?'

'No.'

'Bognor? You were saying last week that was as far as your money would get you this year.'

'Would I pack the Entrovioform for Bognor? Well, the passport at any rate.'

'So you're going abroad.'

'Certainly.'

135

'Working your passage?'

'Don't try to be funny.'

'Give me a clue?'

'I'm not going up the Hindu Kush, and it isn't a fruit-picking holiday in Wisbech. Any more questions?'

'Won't you even tell me?'

'*Especially* you, Marjory. I daren't tell you anything. I told you in confidence the other day that we are down to using two-star petrol in the Rolls, and the next thing I hear is that I've actually been *seen* on a bicycle. You know how tongues wag.'

They were in the forecourt, alongside the car.

'Well,' said Marjory, 'wherever it is, have a nice time.'

Audrey deposited the luggage in the back and got in the driving seat. Brabinger wrestled his pebble glasses over his ears, and got in the passenger seat.

'*A l'aéroport,*' said Audrey, pulling the starter.

'Ah — Germany?' guessed Marjory. 'Give my love to the tsetse fly.'

'Don't be absurd,' Audrey returned. 'They don't have the tsetse fly in Spain.'

'Aha! Spain.'

Audrey was giving nothing away. 'See you at my party.'

The starter motor chattered eagerly, but managed to convey none of its animation to the engine itself.

'What's wrong with this, Brabinger?' Audrey grumbled after a few abortive attempts.

'It's the two-star petrol, madam. She doesn't like it.'

But she lumped it, for no sooner were the car's preferences thus acknowledged when she burst into life, and the old vehicle kicking up the gravel pinked and kangarooed up the drive.

For the summer months, family hour moved out on to the terrace where the Polouvičkas sat on a swing hammock and

136

swayed to and fro. It was the day after the party and DeVere, with his work done for the week, and his social debts paid off and now relaxing in the middle of a heatwave, was at one with the world.

'I know, I might take next week off,' he said.

'Aha — where shall we go?' said his mother.

'What's wrong with here — we can stay here.'

'What is there to do here?'

'You'd be surprised. I was talking to Marjory at the party yesterday, and I thought I might take up a bit of nature study.'

'Why bother your brains?'

'Duty. You know,' DeVere went on, 'till now I regarded the country as a sort of soft cushion to stop the towns bumping into each other and getting damaged. But it really is something in itself.'

'Where did you get such wild ideas?' scoffed the old lady.

DeVere was waxing lyrical: 'You know, man and beast have lived here so long, that each has grown to respect the other in a bond of mutual trust and abiding love, and on days like today, you feel that nothing can destroy that time-honoured relationship.'

They heard a shot — then another — and another. Birds took to the trees, and rabbits and field mice fled. The Polouvičkas looked towards its source which was the top of the drive. Brabinger was back in the old Rolls, which backfired and choked and jerked, and rattled, and steamed down the drive, disappearing behind the trees in the drive to the lodge.

Brabinger was just getting the hang of the controls when he arrived back at the old coach house. Driving was coming back to him.

'Once you learn, you never forget,' he kept telling himself. 'It's like driving a car.'

He managed to stop it and kill the engine, thereby reducing the risk of accident. He got out furtively, went to the coach house door, unlocked it and opened it. He then looked around. Satisfied that the coast was clear, he threw open the rear door to reveal Audrey crouched on the car floor.

He nodded to her. Keeping her head down and holding her hat, she left the car hurriedly and Groucho-Marxed her way into the house.

Brabinger followed her in like manner, carrying the cases. He had been allowed to drive the car and carry the cases in the space of five minutes — revolution must be just round the corner.

He found Audrey in the drawing room, peering over the window sills and drawing the curtains. He put the cases down.

'Thank you, Brabinger,' said Audrey, straightening herself up and recovering her hat. She opened her purse and gave Brabinger a ten pence piece. He looked confused.

'A *pourboire* — a tip,' she explained. 'A nasty habit practised abroad. My ignorant way for lack of the *lingua franca*, of thanking you for a very pleasant drive. Even if it was only from the top of the drive, and I did have to resort to the Kwells.'

Brabinger burbled his incomprehension.

'Quite, quite, Brabinger — and you may well ask why it was necessary to pack these suitcases, plus passport and travellers' cheques to go for a drive in the country.'

'I *was* wondering, madam.'

'I'm on holiday, Brabinger. I shall be spending it here and while I'm here, I shall be sunning myself on the sun-kissed beaches of Spain.'

'I see, madam,' he said, tapping his nose to denote comprehension of which he had none, and complicity, which was what he was paid for. 'You are here but you are in Spain.'

138

'Yes, but the important thing is that while I am here, I am not here.'

'As you wish, madam.'

'At least, I should not be seen.'

'May I ask why?'

'Because I'm in Spain.'

'Of course you are,' he said, trying to chivvy up his straggling thought processes which had yet to catch up with the logic of this conclusion. 'Will you be back for your party, madam?'

'Of course — that's the whole point. The important thing about a holiday is not that one should take one, but that one should be *seen* to have taken one. So until Saturday, I shall remain here and everyone will think I'm abroad.'

Brabinger wasn't happy.

'Don't worry, Brabinger, I've thought this whole thing through. Now, be an angel and run upstairs to the attic. Bring down my husband's old sun-ray lamp.'

'Yes, madam.'

'And the travel box — you know, that old blue trunk we used to throw all our holiday souvenirs in.'

'Yes, madam.'

'Then ring up the airport for the times and flight numbers of today's flights.'

'Yes, madam.'

'Oh, and have a scout round for the old Spanish language records and bring the old seventy-eight gramaphone.'

'Will that be all, madam?'

'Yes, we don't want you run off your feet, do we? You're on holiday.'

After seeing Audrey off, Marjory had wandered up to the post office to buy stamps.

'How do you like the new man up at the manor?' Mrs Patterson asked her, putting down her copy of *Wierd Tales*

139

and separating a cat from a pâté in the deep freeze.

'Mr DeVere? He's very nice.'

'On the surface, yes, but who knows?'

'What do you mean?'

'I only said, who knows — I didn't say I knew anything. But there's things said. Tongues wag and ears flap.'

'What sort of things?'

'They say he's wanted by Interpol.'

'Well, why shouldn't somebody send him flowers...?'

'Interpol — the police.'

Mrs Patterson leant over the counter, her eyeballs rolling like twin-tub bagatelle.

'They say he murdered his wife,' she breathed.

'Wherever did you hear that?' protested Marjory, pulling herself away.

'There's evil. 'Tis in the air. I can feel it in my water.'

'You mustn't believe everything that's in your water, Mrs Patterson, or in your air. Put the thought right out of your mind. He's very sweet.'

'Here's your stamps. Five sevenpenny, that's five, seven — that's fifty-five pence.'

Marjory proffered a fifty, and Mrs Patterson trumped it with three pence. The exchange rate at the Grantleigh post office was still not in tune with Bank of England guidelines.

'Any news of Mrs fforbes-Hamilton?' said the post-mistress.

'She's just gone abroad on her holiday.'

'Is that so? And haven't I just seen her with my own eyes just ten minutes ago.'

'Where?'

'Driving past this very window.'

'That's quite possible — on her way to Exeter airport.'

'And there's me thinking that the airport was the other way from the manor. Still, I expect that's what Constable Peaslake was chasing her on his motorbike to tell her. He was shouting "Remember '47" at the top of his voice.'

Marjory was puzzled.

'I expect that would be her flight number.'

'I hear she's been seeing Mr DeVere again. Friendly again, are they?'

'I don't think that's any of your business, Mrs Patterson,' said Marjory loftily, gathering up her things. 'Good morning.'

As she got to the door, the sinister voice stayed her.

'I wonder who his first victim will be in these parts?'

She turned.

'I don't know. Perhaps you'd like to volunteer.'

At the old lodge, Audrey had already begun her holiday in earnest. She was dressed in a beach robe, and was surrounded by all the props for her holiday production, which Brabinger had brought down from the attic.

'You know, Brabinger,' she said, as he changed the plug on the sun-ray lamp, 'I always say that getting away from it all is all very well, provided you can take a substantial part of it with you. This way, we have all the advantages.'

She shuffled through a sheaf of torn brochures which she'd brought out from the trunk.

'Brown is what used to be red, yellow and green is what used to be green, blue is what used to be black ...' he was muttering to his plug, spitting parings of insulation cable into the fire.

'You're not listening, Brabinger.'

'Sorry, madam.'

'What's more,' she went on, 'once one has arrived, one has so much more time to decide where one's going.' She sat down and reclined in the sun-lounger. 'Now I must decide where I am.' She flicked through the pages.

'Or is the black what used to be blue ...'

'Brabinger, do you see me ...' she quoted her brochure, '...on "sundrenched sands by a glittering sea, where the

141

ancient gods have ordained an eternal spring", or on "rugged hills of almond and olive groves and eagles'-nest villages — the home of Spanish gypsies, and the fiery Flamenco"?'

'Yes, madam.'

'Oh, you're so helpful.'

She got up and went to her suitcase.

'Oh, blow,' she said, rummaging deep into it. 'There's always something, isn't there?'

'What is it, madam?'

'My sunglasses — I appear to have left them at home.'

Within a day, Audrey had worked out a holiday routine. It was not one which involved just lounging about, letting time pass. There was work to be done. The following morning, Brabinger was lured to the door of the drawing room by the sound of a man's voice. He listened.

'*Una Junta Universal, favor, el motor se ha atollado,*' it said in slow dusky tones.

'*Una Junta Universal, favor, el motor se ha atollado,*' Audrey repeated.

He entered to find Audrey sprawled out on the sun-lounger with the language record revolving on the turntable beside her.

'*Una Junta Universal ...*'

'That's what I said, silly man,' Audrey ranted lifting the pickup. 'Yes, Brabinger?'

'Would you like some coffee, madam?'

Audrey referred to her book.

'*Gracias, camarero,*' she said. Then she noticed. She recoiled with horror at the vision of Brabinger before her and sat up. Gone was his formal daydress — the white jacket and the black trousers. Here he stood before her in khaki shorts, an old short-sleeved airtex shirt, a sleeveless pullover with a zig-zag on it, and plimsolls. Nevertheless,

142

he was discharging his duties impeccably.

'Brabinger, what on earth are you doing?'

'Pouring coffee, madam.'

'In those clothes?'

'I understood you were on holiday?'

'So I am, but there is no reason for you to go round looking like a member of the Symbionese Liberation Army.'

'I am creating an illusion, madam.'

'A hallucination, I hope.'

'You see, madam,' explained the erstwhile Beau Brummel of below-stairs, 'it's a well-known fact on the estate what when you are on holiday, I always adopt a more informal mode of dress. If I were seen in my working clothes, people would smell a rat.'

'I see.' She wasn't sure she did, and her look vouchsafed this.

'You did say we were to do this properly or not at all. How can I let you down when you yourself are even taking the trouble to learn the language?'

Audrey relaxed again, and lay back on the sun-lounger with her phrase book.

'Yes,' she said, 'there's nothing like a smattering of the language to lend a touch of authenticity to a story. I shall, of course, be expected to tell a holiday story at my party. Not that I can think of one off-hand which involves being overcharged for a universal joint or asking my way to the lavatory.'

She threw the book down. 'That's all they tell you in these things. By the way, did you find out about my flight?'

'Yes, madam. Two days ago there was a DC 10 Dan-Air Flight 74632, Gate 7, bound for Malaga. There were two stand-by tickets available on it.'

Audrey wrote this down in a notebook which was already well filled with holiday information.

'Thank you,' she said. 'Did they tell you anything else

143

about the flight?'

'Yes, madam. You missed it.'

'But as far as anyone else knows, I was on it, wasn't I? It didn't crash or anything?'

'No, madam.'

'It's just that if it had, it's one of those little details I would have noticed. I don't want to be caught out.'

'May I ask exactly where you are, madam? People have been asking.'

Audrey went to the bureau and pulled out a pile of brochures, from which she extracted one and flicked through its pages, checking the details off with her own notes.

'I am staying in Malaga at the Hotel Balmoral. That's exotic out there, and anyway, it's rather appropriate, I thought. At this moment, I am probably lying on a sun-drenched beach looking at a glittering sea, luxuriating in the eternal spring ordained by ancient gods, and in a moment I shall be on my way up for a lunch of paella and churros, washed down with a glass of Don Cortez.'

Brabinger was impressed.

'Indeed you are, madam,' he said, offering her coffee.

'Thank you. *Expresso favor, camarero.*'

'I beg your pardon, madam?'

'Espresso — all bubbly and frothy like they have it in Spain.'

'Very good, madam,' he raised the coffee pot a good four feet in the air and poured. With a bit of navigation, Brabinger managed to direct the hot brown stream into the cup. It was frothy and bubbly all right.

It was Brabinger's holiday, too, Audrey conceded grudgingly.

Late that evening, just as it was getting dark, Marjory called on DeVere. She was surprised to get the invitation,

144

particularly as she thought he was on holiday. She was pondering over what Mrs Patterson had told her about him in the post office. She did not want to believe anything said against DeVere, but as she looked at the formidable silhouette of the manor, lit by the full moon and heard the distant hoot of an early owl, her credulity gravitated towards the sinister. Why had he invited her — and at this late hour? Mrs Patterson's words 'I wonder who his first victim will be in these parts?' were still richochetting and reverberating round that empty space between her ears.

Yet, drawn by that morbid curiosity which attracts tourists to air-crashes, she kept her appointment.

She need not have feared, which some would say was a pity. DeVere was charm personified.

'Of course, I have an ulterior motive for trying to get to know you a bit — this week, particularly.'

'You mean — with Audrey being away?'

'Yes — there's something you can do for me.'

Oh joy! Marjory knew all along that the holiday trick was to get rid of Audrey. The field was clear. She felt a tingle where a tingle had not been felt for many a long year. 'I wonder who his first victim will be in these parts?' Tingle healed up.

'Oh,' was all she could say.

'I have to take you into my confidence. It's just that I've been hearing certain stories about me which I gather are getting a bit of currency round here. They could make life difficult.'

'What stories?'

'About how I'm some kind of gangster — that I've made my money out of organized crime syndicates, that I'm on the run from the international police. And you haven't heard anything about my late wife, have you?'

'Not a thing — and I don't believe a word of it. Who would start such rumours?'

'That's just it. I can only think of one woman who'd have

145

any reason for doing so.'

'Audrey?'

'Do you have any influence over her?'

'She hangs on my every word.' She got away with it.

'Then do me a favour and see if you can persuade her to cool it. But don't tell her I said anything, of course.'

'I am the soul of discretion.'

'Fine.' The subject was closed. 'Then how about a walk now? It's a fine night.'

Marjory couldn't down her drink quick enough.

'To the woods, then.'

As they went outside, the closed subject opened up again.

'Mr DeVere, you're not *really* a gangster, are you?'

'Why not? Don't I look as if I'm on the run from the police?'

She didn't know whether to believe him or not. He wagged his finger. 'And if Bonnie turns me in, Clyde will be very angry.'

Marjory clasped her hands over her chest and looked skyward.

'Oh, how exciting,' she gasped. 'Just wait till I tell the rector.'

The benison of Marton's old sun-ray lamp was beginning to make its mark on Audrey's flesh. She was a salami-patchwork, a quilt of reds from coral pink to oxblood — her face like a blushing strawberry.

But time was hanging heavy, since fabricating her cover story only took so much of the day, and her solitary confinement which excluded all human contact was hard to bear. True, there was Brabinger for company. But the mistress-servant relationship was so entrenched that their interests and attitudes had evolved in different spheres, which led them both to avoid each other's company rather than to seek it.

The mind, too, has its green baize door with the brass nails, so that their formal relationship could be counted among those vestiges of tradition which persist long after they serve any useful purpose, like cinema curtains. That Audrey was now scantily clad under the sun-ray lamp with goggles on in Brabinger's presence was proof that the ice was beginning to melt. Yet it caused Brabinger as much embarrassment to accept Audrey's invitations to play games to while away the long afternoons, as it abashed her to extend them.

Today, it was the dreaded Scrabble. It was that bad.

'That is not how you spell "icing".' chided Audrey as Brabinger put his third word down on the Scrabble board. 'Icing is spelt with a "c".'

'The word is "ising", madam,' protested the old retainer. 'With an "s". Used to mend decanters with it. Half an ounce of ising in a gill of spirits in a loosely corked vial, then placed in a pipkin surrounded by sand...'

'That's isinglass.'

'Yes, madam. We called it ising.'

'Then it's an abbreviation — I can't allow it.'

'Very good, madam,' he snivelled subserviantly. He re-grouped his letters and put down three.

Audrey craned her neck to read them.

'Nice!' she said, aghast. 'Can't you put "charming"? I have a thing about "nice".'

'I don't have the letters.'

'Then why not put it round that "e" and make it "niece"?'

'Certainly, madam,' he obeyed. 'I score seven, madam,' he said, writing it down on the score sheet.

Audrey was ready with her next move and enthusiastically gathered up a collection of letters and was planting them on the board.

'Good, that clears that treble word score.'

Brabinger inspected her wordplay as she quickly refilled

147

her rack from the bag.

'And what exactly *is* M—A—A—M, madam?'

'It's short for madam,'

'Ma'am short for madam, madam?'

'Yes.'

'An *abbreviation* for madam, madam?'

'Of course.'

'Very good, madam,' he said, writing down a substantial score. Knew his place, did Brabinger. Suddenly Audrey saw the absurdity of her situation.

'I'm bored with this game,' she sighed. 'No, let's face it,' she went on sagging back on the sun-lounger, 'this hasn't been my idea of a holiday.'

And to think it was only up till last year that every August she'd been basking on real silver beaches, and having real exotic meals, and going from villa to villa on an endless whirl of parties. Happy days. She wondered what she'd been doing at precisely that moment last year.

She went to the bureau and took out her five-year diary, and thumbed through its pages.

'According to this, we were just coming to the end of our holiday in Alassio ,' she read on and précied her findings. 'Oh. I was bored stiff. Listen. "Spent evening exchanging addresses with people I hope I'll never see in my life again, and laughing at each other's passport photographs. This morning, we bought a lot of souvenirs, none of which couldn't equally well have been bought in Woolworth's".'

'Then perhaps next year we shall have our holiday in Woolworth's.'

Audrey gave him a withering look. Brabinger withered.

' "Ten stone, one and a half — went to bed," ' Audrey concluded, slamming the diary shut. 'Those were the days, eh?'

'And you don't miss the water till the wells run dry,' Brabinger offered.

Another few minutes had been occupied without

148

recourse to blows. But there were still several days to see off. Brabinger was beginning to take the initiative.

'May I suggest a rehearsal of your story, madam?' he suggested a few days later. 'It is not quite perfect yet, if you'll allow me to say so.'

The story in question was actually one which she was busily adapting for her own purposes, these being to spellbind her guests at her party at the week-end. It concerned an American lady who was going to have been checking into her hotel at the same time as her. She was going to ask the receptionist what time they served breakfast — seven-thirty to ten-thirty came the reply — and what time was lunch? — twelve till two-thirty, she is told. And what time is dinner? — six till nine-thirty, she learns. 'Oh dear, she says, that doesn't leave us much time for sight-seeing!'

Audrey was getting to grips with the story, authenticating it, reeling off all the receptionist's lines in Spanish, reckoning that this was much easier than translating all the tourist's lines into American. Throughout the week, Brabinger had been testing her, and it took until the eve of her 'return' to Grantleigh to perfect it.

'Olé,' exulted Audrey, after a perfect recital. The day had gone quickly and it was just getting dark.

'Well done, madam. That was excellent — I almost believed it myself. Just as well, since it is the performance tomorrow night.'

Audrey was amazed.

'Is it? Good heavens, that means we're flying back tomorrow. Tempus fugit.'

'Yes — I *think* that's the name of the airline, madam.'

'But I can't go back yet — I'm not brown enough. I just have to be a few tones darker. Where's that emergency stuff?'

'What stuff is that, madam?'

'That sun-tan lotion you don't have to have any sun for.'

Brabinger brought forward the salver of lotions and potions, unguents, and liniments. Audrey selected one.

'This is it — a layer of this and tomorrow I'll be Ella Fitzgerald, colour-wise. I say, Brabinger, would you do my back?'

Brabinger was shocked. The green baize door had slipped a hinge. Do her back, rub ointment into my lady's back? Yet Audrey seemed quite matter-of-fact about it.

'But madam,' spluttered the old man, 'do you really think I ought?'

'I can't, can I? Not without slipping a disc.'

Brabinger was agape and refused to take the little plastic bottle.

'Now don't stare at it like that. It won't bite you.'

'But, madam, as butler, this is not really within the province of my duties.'

'Of course it is. It's in a bottle and there's bound to be some alcohol in it somewhere. Now, don't be so feeble.'

'Very well, madam.'

He took the bottle limply in his fingers. Audrey spread herself out face down on the sun-lounger. Brabinger was shaking the bottle in his hand.

'You have to take the top off.'

He did so, and palmed some of the ointment. He was almost in tears. He was about to apply it to the prostrate body, when from out in the garden they heard the gate slam.

They both looked up. There were voices, too. One was DeVere's.

'I feel a bit hesitant about going through Audrey's garden — and I've been through minefields,' DeVere was saying.

The other was Marjory.

'Who cares?' she laughed. 'She's away and Brabinger is as deaf as a post. He only hears bells.'

Brabinger and Audrey rushed to the window, turning out

150

all the lights on the way. They were in time to see DeVere and Marjory heading from the gate into the woods at the back of the old lodge.

'Come on,' Marjory was heard to say. 'It'll be too late in a minute.'

DeVere's eager, 'I can't wait,' came faintly through the pines and hung in the air.

Audrey was numbed and closed the curtain. Brabinger put on the light.

'What on earth's going on?' demanded Audrey. 'I thought DeVere was on holiday.'

'No, madam — I understand he has been having his holidays here.'

'You knew that and you didn't tell me?'

'Yes and no, madam.'

'What do you mean, yes and no?'

'Yes, I did know, and no, I didn't tell you. I didn't want to upset your holiday.'

'Well, that's one thing,' said Audrey, the timbre of her voice sharpening and rising. 'But what in heaven's name are he and Marjory going down to the woods for?'

'That's the other thing, madam.'

'What other thing?'

'The other thing I didn't tell you, for the same reasons. You see, I had seen them going down to the woods every day this week, at this time.' He began to falter.

'Go on,' Audrey coaxed him.

'And they came out about an hour later ... brushing the grass off themselves.'

'And you didn't tell me?' screamed Audrey.

Brabinger stammered something inaudibly.

'Really, the minute my back is turned. This is unthinkable. DeVere and Marjory! Oh, I knew she was after him, but I would have credited him with better taste. Would you say she was attractive, Brabinger?'

'It would depend on the lighting, madam.'

She marched into the hall, kicking off her flip-flops and began to substitute coat and gumboots for beachwear.

'This liaison must stop at once. I'll just have to go down there and break it up.'

She was back in the drawing room making a beeline for the french window when Brabinger restrained her in a manner within the limits of his station and his hand full of suntan oil.

'If I may say so, madam, that would be most unwise — not to say, improbable.'

'Is it, indeed?' she snapped.

'Yes, madam — you're away in Spain. If you were to appear now, they would know you hadn't been away.'

Audrey's emotion abated and gave way to reason. Brabinger was right. She had worked out all her flight times.

'What a time to be stuck in this squalid little country. Just wait till tomorrow. I'll have something to say to Marjory and her Lothario.'

She regained her composure.

'Carry on, Brabinger,' she said, handing him the suntan oil and spread-eagling herself on the sun-lounger.

Brabinger knelt by her side and began to search her back for a suitable place to apply it. He made contact.

'Come on now, stroke me — as if I was a cat.'

'But, madam ...'

'Harder. Oh, if it hurts your professional pride, shut your eyes and think of England. God knows I had to. Think of Spain if you like. What about some music?'

Brabinger was glad of a moment's respite to put a record on. It was Flamenco guitar music. He hung the task out as long as possible, but was all too soon back in position at Audrey's side. He hovered over her back, not daring to touch the pink shoulders.

'Come on, Brabinger, grasp the nettle,' Audrey entreated him, as if exhorting a lacrosse team to greater efforts. 'We'll

152

never make the centrefold spread of *The Tatler* at this rate.'

Brabinger took her at her word, and threw himself into the task. No lily-limbed lacrosse team, he.

DeVere and Marjory were emerging from the wood brushing themselves down.

'I hope you weren't too disappointed.'

'No — perhaps we'll have better luck tomorrow night.'

'I'll be saying good night, then.'

'Good night.'

They parted, Marjory going off across the paddock, and DeVere skipping over the gate into the garden of the old lodge.

It was a lovely night for a saunter back to the manor. He looked up at the stars, picking out the Plough, the Orion's belt and sword, and the W of Cassiopeia. Such are the imponderables of time and space, that he was looking at the star Betelgeuse, and what he saw was a twinkle as it had been at the time of the Battle of Hastings. It was the sort of concept which made a mockery of the time it takes to get from Central London to the westward motorway on a Friday evening. The air was still and the faint thrum of Flamenco guitar music waxed and waned like the twinkling of the stars.

DeVere was so absorbed in the wonders of the multi-dimensional universe above him, that the incompatibility of Spanish music on a Somerset farm did not at once register. But when it did, he followed it. It led to the window of the old lodge.

He crept up to it and peered in.

What is one to think when you see a lady such as Audrey laying face down on a sun-bed with her bra strap loosened,and her ancient retainer beating out Flamenco rhythms with his hands on her back.

Even DeVere's normally resourceful mind could only think of one explanation.

153

Audrey looked magnificent in her evening dress, the duck-egg blue one with the leg-of-mutton sleeves and the sequined neckline. And its pale colouring seemed to make a feature of her skin of 'Burnt Sienna'. The party was in full swing. Apart from the more subdued surrounding, the party, its people and its conversation were indistinguishable from the party at the manor the week before. The women who had been at DeVere's party in short dresses had taken their lead from the others, and come to Audrey's party in long. Those who had been long, were now in short. The other difference was Audrey herself.

She was now in her element, charming, witty, elegant, and gracious to a fault. And her story had been going down so well.

DeVere was standing on his own, wondering how this Portland stone inglenook had appeared where he distinctly remembered there being a different fireplace, but he was enjoying Audrey's bluff.

'I was having breakfast at the Hotel Balmoral in Malaga ... there was this American lady ... and the camarero, that's the waiter, said ... *El desayuno* ... that's breakfast ... *las ocho hasta las once.*' It was a brilliant performance.

'... oh dear, that doesn't leave us much time for sight-seeing,' elicited the gust of guffaws Audrey had anticipated.

'Oh, I could have died,' Audrey hooted.

Marjory arrived, her entrance wiping the smile off Audrey's face.

'Hello, Audrey,' she said, 'had a nice time?'

Audrey scowled at her.

'Yes, thank you, Marjory. I'm a new woman.' Then pointedly, 'I gather the same could be said of you.' On Audrey swept to her next engagement, which appeared to be with Arnold. It looked like he had achieved his 'Deep Caramel'.

'Hello, Audrey. You're certainly looking better.'

'Yes, I am, thank you. I'm feeling wonderful. The

holiday was simply heaven.'

'Where were you?'

Out came the cover story.

'Malaga. You know — sun-drenched sands on a glittering sea. It was almost as if ancient gods had ordained an eternal spring.'

Like hell they did.

'Huh! All that rain!' said Arnold. 'We were there, too. Got this under the sun-ray lamp. Doesn't look the same — you can always tell. We were at the Hotel Balmoral. Where were you?'

Audrey faltered slightly, but imperceptibly.

'I was at the Hotel Flamingo.'

'But I thought you said you were at the Balmoral,' said a trouble-maker from Audrey's last audience.

Audrey's mind was racing to keep ahead.

'I didn't actually *stay* there. I went there for the odd meal. They do the best Albondigas soup in all Spain.'

'For breakfast?'

'I didn't see that on the menu,' said Arnold.

'You obviously weren't there when I was there. You must have been on the beach, charring yourself into "Deep Caramel"...' she held her arm to his cheek to compare their tans '... or was it "Whippet Beige"?'

DeVere couldn't resist the sport, and strolled over to join them. Audrey saw him coming and took evasive action, but the room was too full for an escape. She was caught.

'I must say, Audrey, you do look much better. Do you feel better?'

'I do — I expect you do, to. Where did you go if it's not a rude question?'

'I stayed here. It was great. Where did you say *you* were?'

'Malaga — it's in Spain.'

'Is that so? Now, there's a funny thing. I have a villa there. If I'd known, you could have stayed there, at least for the time being while they cleared up after the fire at the

155

Flamingo.'

Audrey gulped.

'That would have been nice. Where did you say your villa was?'

'You know the little church of St Maria on the Avienda del Albatros?'

Audrey's 'yes' meandered over two octaves and four syllables.

'It takes you up under the aqueduct. It's the first village you come to at the top of the avenue in the mountains.'

'Of course, yes. In the rugged hills of almond and olive groves — the home of Spanish gypsies and the fiery Flamenco. Don't you think Malaga is beautiful?'

DeVere moved in for the kill.

'Oh, did you say Malaga? I thought you said Marbella.'

'Oh, isn't it funny how one eagle's-nest village looks very much like another? Have you had some *cruditées?*'

Greased as Audrey's body was, she had no right to slip out of trouble that easily, he thought.

She was saved by a commotion which erupted the other side of the room. Brabinger appeared to be at the bottom of it. He was being ribbed by Arnold.

'Been hearing about you, Brabinger, old man, what? Know what I mean, attaboy, eh?'

'And at your age, too,' said another. 'Didn't think you had it in you,' echoed a colleague.

'You old rogue, you. Life in the old dog yet, eh?'

Brabinger was being slapped on the back and buffeted from all sides, and was desperate to keep his tray of drinks on an even keel.

Audrey looked across the room, demanding an explanation.

'Oh, haven't you heard?' said DeVere.

'Heard what?'

'There may be nothing in it,' he teased.

'In what, for heaven's sake?'

'You know how tongues wag.'

'What have they been saying?'

The perspiration of panic began to stand out on Audrey's brow and her colours began to run.

'It's not really for me to say,' DeVere went on, 'but while you were away, Brabinger had a woman in the house — you know, a bit of ... hanky-panky.'

'I beg your pardon?'

Brabinger staggered across the room towards them.

'Brabinger, is this true?'

'I don't know, madam, but I appear to be the object of some ribaldry.'

Audrey for the prosecution.

'While I was away, is it true that you were having some ...humpty dumpty?'

'Hanky-panky,' corrected DeVere.

'That is to say, were you entertaining a lady in the house?'

DeVere came to the rescue.

'Like I said, it's just an idle rumour. I mean it could have been his niece for all we know.'

Audrey nodded at Brabinger.

'Yes, sir, it was my niece.'

'Your *great*-niece, Brabinger, of course,' half-agreed Audrey.

'My sister's daughter ... Stephanie,' added Brabinger.

A good touch, that, thought DeVere.

'*Grand*-daughter,' she said. 'Of course, I remember you asked whether she could come and spend a few days from London. It had completely slipped my mind — that Spanish sun, you know. How *is* Stephanie, Brabinger?'

Brabinger excelled himself with 'As beautiful as ever, madam.'

DeVere now edged in.

'I agree,' he said.

This startled Audrey and her eyes narrowed and bored into DeVere as he went on, 'I thought Brabinger's niece was

157

very beautiful. Rather like you, in fact. From what I saw.'

Audrey tried to change the subject.

'Do have some more of this Spanish wine,' she offered, taking a bottle from Brabinger's salver. 'After all, it isn't every bottle you drink that's duty free.'

'Not from Sainsbury's, no,' said DeVere declaring himself. Then he added, 'Don't you think that you're sailing a bit close to the wind ... Stephanie?'

Audrey was pouring the wine, edging the stream of wine further away from the glass, obliging DeVere to move away from the group of onlookers.

'How much do you know?' she hissed, through clenched teeth, which with a minimal lip movement was transformed into a smile for the benefit of her guests. 'What have you seen?'

'Not a lot — I mean, the place was so cluttered up with guide books, brochures, sun-ray lamps ...'

'Peeping Tom,' she sneered.

She grabbed his arm with her mortice-lock grip of which Otto Chubb would have been proud, and steered him through the crowd and on to the terrace, before she released her hold.

'All right! Now, let's have it. What are you saying?'

DeVere was cool.

'Only that you spent your holidays on the Costa del Grantleigh.'

Audrey sighed, turned, walked to the end of the terrace with her hands to her temples, and walked back.

'We have to be mature about this,' she said soberly. 'You realize that if this gets out, it could ruin me? I'd be the laughing stock of the estate.'

'Yes.' said DeVere, unabashed and with no signs of relenting. 'You know how tongues wag.'

'If this is blackmail, what have I got to do to make you keep quiet?'

'Nothing.'

'What?'

'Nothing. Nothing that is, except keep quiet about a few things yourself.'

'What do you mean?'

'You seem to have control of the bush telegraph round here, and certain stories about me, about my late wife, about my source of income. That Interpol are after me?'

Audrey showed no signs of recognizing these stories.

'These rumours have to start somewhere,' he said with scorn.

'And are you saying *I'm* spreading these rumours?'

'Yes — at my party last week.'

Audrey tested her memory. 'I said nothing against you at the party. As I remember, all I said was that you didn't live on a Milk Marketing Board subsidy. Though I can't think why Interpol should be after you for that.'

'Well, tongues wag.'

'Why should they?'

'To show that they're happy, maybe.'

'And it certainly isn't me who lubricates them.'

DeVere was not expecting such a flagrant denial, and adopted a conciliatory tone.

'Now, if any of these rumours were true — well, that's fair game.'

Audrey saw her chance.

'So-ho. You've no objection to me going round telling people about *your* little escapades. Your romance?'

'What romance?'

'Oh, heartless brute — that you use a woman so cruelly and then *forget!*' declaimed Audrey, turning on the drama.

'What are you talking about?'

'Your little moonlight trysts with Marjory Frobisher, that's what!'

'But it was just ...'

'It doesn't matter what it *was*. It's what it *looked* like. The fact is, I saw you with my own eyes ... well, I saw you with

Brabinger's actually — every night this week. You were seen coming out of these woods, yes, brushing yourself down. It would cause an awful scandal if that got out. I can hear Mrs Patterson saying, "Good heavens, Marjory Frobisher! He must be desperate." And you know that tongues wag.'

'Especially Mrs Patterson's, eh?'

'Yes — of course. Familiarize yourself with the neighbourhood before you go making wild accusations.'

'All right, all right. You drive a hard bargain. So we have a stalemate. A truce.'

'I think we do.'

'All right, do I have to sign something?'

'I don't think that will be necessary. Now if you'll excuse me, I have guests to entertain.'

DeVere blocked her path. 'Wouldn't you like to know what we were doing in the woods?'

'Certainly not. The mind boggles.'

'It was all quite innocent. Come on, I'll show you.'

He grabbed her hand and ran her off the terrace to the garden gate and into the woods. Plaintive cries of 'This is most improper', 'Have you no scruples?' and 'We might be seen' could clearly be heard above the chatter at the party in the house.

Once deep in the woods, DeVere slackened his pace, and motioned Audrey to hush. He knelt down by the side of the woodland path and slowly crawled up the bank, beckoning Audrey to follow. She did so, reluctantly. At the top of the bank, they lay on the flat and wriggled across to where the undergrowth thickened. Then they saw them.

A badger's head appeared out of the bushes and made its way cautiously out into the middle of a clearing which was bathed in moonlight. Another followed. Then the two cubs crept out of hiding and romped in the open space.

Audrey's mood changed at once. She was fascinated. She didn't move for ten full minutes. By the time she looked up,

160

DeVere was back down at the bottom of the bank. She got up and followed him, using tree roots for handholds, and steps. They were out of the woods before they spoke.

'Badgers,' said Audrey. 'You and Marjory were just looking at badgers?'

'An orgy of badger-watching. She's been giving me a crash-course on your local wildlife, familiarizing myself with the neighbourhood, you might say. Apparently, it's not my strongest point,'

Audrey was almost ashamed of herself. In fact, she was ashamed of Brabinger. He'd put the thought into her head.

'You must admit,' she said by way of mitigation, 'that when you see two people — a man and a woman coming out of the woods in the moonlight, brushing themselves down, you aren't going to think they're playing croquet, are you?'

As they came out of the woods, a cloud passed and they were spotlighted by a moonbeam.

'You could have got yourself involved in a frightful scandal. You're lucky it was only me who saw you.'

They were brushing themselves down, and then each other.

'I mean ...' said Audrey, stopping dead in her tracks, and looking at the old lodge. The entire party had spilled out on to the lawn and were lining the fence by the garden gate to get a good view of the couple as they emerged from the woods.

Audrey tried to look as if she had been playing croquet.

'You were saying?' said DeVere.

'I was going to say — you know how tongues wag.'

A lot of tongues were already doing so.

6

The rumour of the romance spread around the estate and via Grantleigh to Marlbury. Indeed, it went further and got a column inch in the *Daily Mail* 'Diary'. Did they have 'plans' it wanted to know. All gossip column people seemed required to have 'plans'.

Audrey resented the additional pressure on her — the jibes, the jokes, the knowing looks and the becks and wreathed smiles, and above all, the 'understanding' which she now had to deal with. But she still denied it vigorously and did nothing to moderate her line of invective against DeVere.

But her own private and social life was lying in ruins. The money was running out fast. The bills were coming faster than she could pay them. She had already twice had occasion to go foraging in the bottom of drawers for working capital in minted form.

On the practical side, Marjory kept reminding her that she had to get a job. On the social side after the personal fiasco of her cocktail party, much social ground had to be regained. But apart from DeVere, nobody knew about the faked holiday, so that was something. But the problem got more acute. It was this; the faster her own resources ran out, the more essential it became to make it with DeVere, but the harder it became to appear to keep up with him.

It came to a head one breakfast in the late summer.

Audrey was reading her *Daily Mail*.

162

'I see Lord Mortlake is allowing Harborough Hall to be used for an advertisement for paint,' she reported to Brabinger, who was serving a grapefruit.

'It's too frightful. That we're reduced to the level of performing seals to survive. I suppose a paint advertisement is better than having it taken over by the NUR or turning it into a health farm.'

'Maybe with Mr DeVere, madam, we got off lightly.'

'I didn't say that. It's the thin end of the wedge. You know, I'm not sure I like this insidious emasculation of the aristocracy. I honestly think I'd prefer to hear the honest rumble of tumbril on cobble and have a rabble waving placards at the top of the drive. At least Marie Antoinette knew where she stood.'

She sighed and looked thoughtful.

'Come to think of it, "let then eat cake" was a pretty inane remark even by French Salon standards.' She paused. 'Unless, of course, *she* was advertising something — at least that's something I've never stooped to.'

'*Que sera, sera,* madam,' mused Brabinger, apropos of nothing very much, which Audrey very properly identified as the motto of the Bedfords.

'Mind you, I'm not sure I like the way our lot is carrying on. According to Nigel Dempster, there's been another outbreak of walnut throwing at Queen Charlotte's ball dinner parties. It's appalling. In our day, it used to be rolls. Perhaps I shall write another letter to *The Times*.'

'Another letter?' asked Brabinger.

'Yes — don't you remember my highly regarded contribution to the controversial "Milk on tea is first" debate in 1965?'

'As if it were yesterday, madam,' fawned Brabinger, placing the morning mail on the salver on the sideboard. She recognized the sound.

'Typed, handwritten, brown or white?'

Brabinger shuffled through the pile of letters. 'Two

brown with window envelopes, three brown without, which look like bills ...'

'You know what you can do with them. Just give me the white handwritten ones — they're personal.'

'There aren't any, madam.'

Brabinger took the pile of letters and flicked them one by one into the elephant's foot wastepaper basket.

'Bill from the garage, bill from the Electricity Board — red — a card from the GPO saying we are to be disconnected forthwith — one from the Gas.'

'Don't bother — they all say the same. "If this bill has already been paid, please ignore this notice within seven days".'

'... a bill from Mason's the grocer,' Brabinger went on.

'Just a minute — I paid that last week.'

She took the offending envelope, opened it and read it. She wished she hadn't. The nub of the letter was that her cheque had bounced and that credit facilities were being withdrawn forthwith. Brabinger guessed something of the sort, and Audrey confirmed it with, 'Well, I suppose they do have to look to their customers to bail them out of their financial difficulties.'

'Do you intend to write them a stinker, madam?'

'No — it's gauche to argue with tradesmen.'

'One from the bank,' announced Brabinger. It was a statement at which Audrey flinched perceptibly.

'And a covering letter,' She read it. Let's be honest. She was broke.

'Nothing serious, I hope, madam?'

'No — the bank manager's quite right, as usual — it *isn't* for him to tell me how I should economize. Anyway, we are economizing,' she said as an afterthought as she lifted the lids of the silver dishes before her.

'I think I'll just have the kedgeree this morning. Give the kidneys to Bertie.'

'... and one large white from County Hall — stiff,' came

164

the fair description of the item Brabinger was handing to her.

Audrey dropped the lid back on the dish. Stiff? This could only be one thing — an invitation. Not *an* invitation — *the* invitation. It must be to the social highlight of the county season — the Lord Lieutenant's charity gala. She eagerly tore open the envelope and looked at the embossed white card with its serrated gilt edges. The first thing her eye picked out was the hard facts of modern life. It was £35 a ticket. The second was an even harder fact of modern life.

'Since when has my name been Richard DeVere?' she said, angrily, checking the invitation with the envelope and showing them to Brabinger.

'Oh, I'm sorry, madam,' said Brabinger, mortified at the *faux pas*. 'I didn't notice — oh, the postman did say that Mr DeVere had one the same. Perhaps he has got yours. Shall I call at the manor?'

'No, don't. I don't think I want to go this year,' she lied. 'It's the same year in and year out. I want to do something new — something different.' With this impassioned vision of a great and glorious future, Audrey concerned herself with the day's domestic details. Brabinger awaited his instructions.

'First, I want to ring up Mason's with my grocery order.'

'I did, madam, only...'

'Didn't they accept it?'

'I don't know, madam. The phone has been cut off.'

'You see, they can't even pay their phone bills. I told you they were in deep financial water. So we'd better go elsewhere.'

She wracked her brains.

'Tell you what — why don't we, just once, just for a change, just for the hell of it, do our shopping at that place opposite Mason's?'

'The supermarket, madam?'

'Is that what it's called? Yes, let's go there.'

165

Audrey's mind was racing along its own devious route, a cerebral spaghetti-junction. Yes, she could pretend the bank's letter didn't come till the afternoon post, which left her time to bounce just one more cheque — or maybe two. But what then? Cash in hand was now the *cause célèbre*. Something else had to be sold. The car? It was no good her hoping that these thoughts were secret.

Years of living in proximity had endowed Brabinger with the ability to divine the meaning of every inflection of the voice, every shift of the eye, and every gesture, with a 99 per cent success rate. To him, her little signs were as clear as if spelt out in ten-foot neon letters. More often than not, he was way ahead of her.

This was one of the more often occasions, and he knew what was coming next and dreaded it.

'Is the car clean?' Audrey asked casually.

Brabinger knew that the car — his beloved Rolls, his charge and companion for thirty years — was now bound for the market place. Audrey, possessed of much the same interpretive skills as Brabinger, read anguish in his eyes, which was belied by his emotionless reply.

'The car is never dirty, madam. You know the love and care I lavish on your vehicle.'

'Yes — I do. But I just want it to look its very best.'

In the nick of time, it occurred to Brabinger that there was just one thing, which might bring about a reprieve.

'Indeed, it will, madam. For the Lord Lieutenant's charity gala, I presume?'

Audrey lost heart. She couldn't tell him that the car was for sale. Neither could she find the courage to tell herself that the social delights of the gala at £35 a ticket were to be forfeit. Nor indeed had she the face to show up there with anything less than her traditionally extravagant style. There had to be another way.

'Yes — certainly, the charity gala, Brabinger. What else?'

Breakfast at the manor that day was an equally businesslike affair. On one side of the round table, set to catch the sun through the oriel in the morning room, sat DeVere. He was going through his post, and was already dictating his answers into a pocket-recorder, ready for his secretary Hilda's arrival at his office. At the other side of the table sat Mrs Polouvička who was reading the paper.

'I see Lord Mortlake is using Harborough Hall to advertise paint,' mumbled the old lady through a mouthful of toast.

DeVere did not answer.

'Letter to Dr Tanaguchi, Hilda. I want to sign this one personally. Dr Yoshiaki Tanaguchi, House of Perpetual Serenity and Moral Fibre, Dock Street, Osaka, Japan. Dear Dr Tanaguchi — thank you for your confirmation ... of further supplies of blow fish ...'

'Bedrich,' interrupted his mother.

'Sssh! Thank you for your confirmation ...'

'Bedrich. Isn't Lord Mortlake the man with the flighty wife?'

'Oh, do be quiet,' said DeVere firmly but patiently, his mind in the Orient where the old are venerated. He spoke back into his recorder.

'No, not you, Hilda. Don't write that, write this ... thank you for your confirmation ...'

'Bedrich.'

'Mother!'

'You are in a tizzy-wizzy today, aren't you?'

'I am *not* in a tizzy-wizzy.' He spoke into the machine. 'Excuse me, Hilda — over and out.'

He switched off. 'At least, I wasn't until you started interrupting.'

'Who got out of bed the wrong side this morning?'

'It wasn't me.'

'Then who was it? Some piece you won't introduce to your mother?'

167

'Mother, I sleep alone. I don't know what you think I am.'

'I know you are too old to need a charabanc.'

'The word is chaperone.'

'But you can't always be trusted. Now, what is wrong with that nice Audrey?'

'Plenty! She makes life very difficult at times.'

'And at other times?'

'She makes it worse. All right, there are times when I think differently, but I'm not prepared to discuss it on an empty stomach.'

'I've been thinking, isn't it time you invited her out — a woman likes a nice straight honest approach — never mind all this manoeuvring. Ask her straight out, "Will you or won't you?"'

'Mother, don't be disgusting.'

'Well, it's time we had results.'

'Will you let me lead my own life!'

'They're all talking about you two down at the Beetle Drive. So you are too slow with her. So she gets herself snapped up by some randy old duke on a last fling, like Lord Mortlake: you should care, huh?'

'That's not on the cards. She likes this place too much. These old English families are like runner beans — they only flourish if tied to a stake. Away from here she's nobody, she withers and dies.'

'Well, Princess Anne is spoken for. And you are getting on in years yourself, so you can't expect an oil painting.'

'I have some oil paintings.'

'But they don't have connections. They couldn't get you into the Phyllis Court at the Henley Regatta.'

'You don't have to sell Audrey to me. Now will you stop match-making, please? For all you know, I might have other plans.'

'Who?'

DeVere threw a 'wouldn't-you-like-to-know' glance and

168

resumed speaking into his buttered recorder.

'Dear Dr Tanaguchi ...'

'Who? She's a doctor?' exulted the old lady.

'Oh, Mother, do stop.'

She had seen an invitation in the pile of letters, reached over the table, retracted it, and read it.

'Why don't you take her to the Lord Whatsit's Gala?'

'What?'

'This — Lord High and Mighty's charity do.'

'Because I'm not invited. That's for her. Besides, if I asked her she wouldn't accept. Not from me, and she won't until she has to. Mind you, she's going downhill fast now and she can't hold out much longer. I'm biding my time. Besides, I'm doing very nicely without her.'

The old lady's eyes narrowed.

'What do you mean?'

'Didn't I tell you? There's a television company doing a series on old English houses and their old English owners. You know — great British families. They're doing one on me.'

Mrs Polouvička leapt up in excitement.

'You? They think we're an old English family?'

'As the hills.'

'They're doing a TV show on us?'

'*Me*. It's a television commercial. For Fontleroy's Old English Tonic.'

He went over to the sideboard and selected a little bottle from a silver tray. 'You know — "the Little Aristocrat".' He cocked his nose as a gesture of superiority — the product's advertising gimmick.

'Never mind what it is — so long as it's you on television,' exclaimed the old lady skipping into the hall and reappearing with a clothes brush.

'My boy on television,' she clucked on, belabouring his shoulders with the brush. 'I've always wanted my boy in show business. To be an actor — to be a film star.'

169

'They don't want acting. They want me to be me — my little aristocratic self — this fine example of the English landed gentry.'

The old lady was solemn.

'We fooled 'em, eh?'

'We have arrived, don't you think ... and without Audrey. And isn't this our chance to tell the world?'

'Good boy. We've come a long way, you and I?' she said thoughtfully. 'To think nobody could tell I'm not a duchess.' She resumed her sartorial assault with the clothes brush.

'You must look smart, my boy. You haven't been in the films since the evacuation, and then you weren't looking your best.' She checked his quota of handkerchiefs. 'One for show, and one for blow.'

DeVere objected.

'Mother, would you please stop treating me like a kid?'

The old lady's pounding subsided, and she stood back to admire her son.

'I'm sorry, Bedrich. I mean, Richard.'

DeVere approved of the change of name.

'Why, thank you. At last you take me seriously.'

His mother went back to her place at table and sat down huffily.

'Eat your grapefruit,' she ordered.

Audrey and Brabinger were skulking round the Marlbury supermarket. What both were aware of, but neither dared mention, was that the man who was about to have a cheque bounced on him was Richard DeVere, the owner of this supermarket. Neither could understand it, but they appeared to be drawing attention to themselves. What could be more natural than a man and a woman walking through a supermarket, she in cape and tweed hat with a pheasant feather and he, pushing the trolley in his thick, pebble glasses, a chauffeur's cap and leather gaiters?

From the minute they drew up at the entrance in the shooting brake, and Brabinger slipped out of the passenger side to open the door for her, the driver, they seemed to have been the object of more than cursory appraisal.

'Aren't these places wonderful?' Audrey enthused. 'Look, there's some *pâté de fois gras*. It seems you can get absolutely everything.'

The trolley, which Brabinger was wrestling with in an attempt to get all four wheels going in the same direction, was already full, yet Audrey appeared to be laying in for a siege. Her mound of groceries was crested by a six-pack of Fontleroy's Old English Tonic. She kept seeing more things she wanted.

'Would you turn round a minute, Brabinger,' she said catching sight of some unspecified requisite in the household goods department. Brabinger obliged, and Audrey took advantage of his averted gaze to avail herself of a bumper four-pack lavatory roll bargain, which she thrust deep into the bowels of her trolley.

'And something for Bertie,' she muttered and cast her eyes about in search for something in the doggy line. She saw a tin of dog meat and helped herself. One of the unwritten laws of supermarket life is that you don't help yourself from other people's trollies. This Audrey had just done, not that she would have been aware of it, had not a voice of protest been raised from the other side of the alley.

'Excuse me, that's mine,' it said.

It belonged to Ned — old Ned of Grantleigh, the old Ned who had worked on the estate for longer than anybody cared to remember.

'Oh, hello, Ned — what brings you here?' said Audrey.

'My dog meat,' he said, reclaiming it.

'I'm sorry,' said Audrey, 'I mean, what brings you to the supermarket?'

'The freshest meat and the best vegetables in the whole of

171

Marlbury.'

'Except for the Grantleigh estate,' she chipped in.

'*Including* the Grantleigh estate, ma'am,' Ned emphasised.

Audrey looked in his trolley and pulled out a bundle of kindling wood.

'What's this doing in here?' she asked.

'Best kindling in the world, that. It's tarred.'

'But Ned, you have the run of the estate, surely you don't *buy* ...' Her words faded at the sight of a packet of frozen peas deeper in his trolley.

'Don't you grow your own peas?'

'Not as good as them, ma'am. They're as advertised on television.'

'On the television?'

'Yes, ma'am. They're big and juicy. They look wunnerful on a twenty-four inch screen.'

'A twenty-four inch screen?'

'Yes, and so lovely and ripe and green.'

'Green? Do you have a *colour* television?'

'Of course, ma'am.'

'What will they think of next?'

Only Audrey could have made the next remark sound relevant to the last. 'But you live in a *tied* cottage, Ned. A rent-free subsidized cottage at Mellow End Mill.'

'Ah, but it don't affect reception, ma'am. The Ilcaster transmitter beams a picture right through the valley.'

'But you have your own garden, Ned.' Without any form of farewell, Audrey walked away down the aisle, bemused. 'I give up,' she confided to Brabinger.

'Ned, whose cucumbers always win at the flower show, *buying* vegetables, because they look good — on television. Doesn't he know they're dyed — like the kippers?'

She dwelt a moment on Ned's traditional position on the estate.

'What's happened to the lovely old tied cottage? As I

172

remember it, Mellow End Mill used to have that beautifully quaint old earth closet and the little plaque saying, 'Oh God, thou seest me'. So picturesque. Really, the whole fabric of society is on its head. It's that policeman son of his that's been giving Ned ideas.'

Audrey saw the mechanic's wife turning the corner into the alley which they were now blocking. She slipped into the deep-freeze section.

'Not that I mind being seen by anyone, of course,' she said to Brabinger by way of mitigation for a rather abrupt dash. 'Where do we go from here?'

'The check-out counter, madam,' He pointed. Audrey's gaze followed his finger to the check-out, and beyond to a group of people by the exit.

'Isn't that Polly, the gamekeeper's girl? Oh, Lor there's Mrs Styles from the dairy.'

She retreated to the cover of a pile of bargain sugar.

'Once more round the block, Brabinger.'

They set off again.

The drawing room commanded a good view of the forecourt of the manor, and one of the most scenic aspects of the estate. It was, therefore, this part of the house which was chosen for the set for the Fontleroy's Tonic commercial. In charge of the host of technicians and make-up people who prowled about the house, trailing cables from vans parked outside and taking light and sound readings, was the director, Bernie Maggs — a chubby man in a powerful aftershave lotion and crocodile shoes. He had had the breakfast table taken away and replaced with a high-backed Jacobean chair and a small side table.

Here DeVere was to sit and say his lines endorsing 'the Little Aristocrat'.

'Okay, so you have come into the manor,' said Maggs, 'and we've seen the outside of the house and the grounds.

Now, you've come in here as if for a day at the races — just like Rex Harrison in "The Yellow Rolls-Royce". You come into the room here and sit down in the chair. On the table beside you will be the product.'

The way he said 'the product' was dismissive, leaving one in no doubt that he didn't care whether it was Fontleroy's Tonic or a washing-up liquid.

'Then you say ...' he handed DeVere a script and pointed to the relevant passage.

DeVere read, ' "There are some things we British can always be proud of. Our beautiful country houses, for instance. But you don't have to own a house like this to preserve the traditional flavour of English life".'

'Then you fix yourself a drink and pour in a splash of product. Go on.'

DeVere continued. ' "Fontleroy's Old English Tonic — the Little Aristocrat".'

'Then,' went on Maggs, 'While you're drinking, you say, "Just add a touch of class".'

'I'm not a ventriloquist.'

'Well, I'll say it then. Or you say it and I'll drink it. All you have to do is look the part. You know — imposing. But I don't have to tell you how to look classy, do I?'

DeVere liked this, but still sought reassurance.

'You did say that you'd also asked the Duke of Bedford and the Marquis of Bath and Lord Salisbury to do this?'

'Sure, sure,' said Maggs.

'And how did *they* do it?'

'I don't know — they turned it down.'

Audrey had got to the supermarket check-out. She was fascinated to see how it all worked — the conveyor belt, the totals being rung up on the till, automatic receipts, and the grooved arm which led to a scoop on the change dispenser.

Her basket was emptying fast as Polly, who had worked

at the manor in her time, was not anxious to detain Audrey longer than necessary. A queue was forming behind them which consisted of Ned, Mrs Styles from the dairy, and they were just being joined by the rector.

As the basket emptied, Audrey could see her pack of lavatory rolls protruding, and lest Brabinger, Ned and the others saw it, held out her elbow so that the basket was enveloped by the wing of her cape. She didn't much like the idea of Polly seeing it either, but trusted her professional discretion which must surely have bound her to secrecy about all sorts of horrors in her time.

Quelle horreur! The pack was in Polly's hands and she was scrutinizing it in vain for a price. Then to Audrey's utter amazement, she rang the bell on the side of the till, held the pack aloft for all to see, and yelled at the top of her voice —

'How much the bumper toilet rolls?'

Audrey went bright red and forced an ingratiating smile at her audience, which seemed to swell by the second as more Midionites appeared to be crawling from every shelf.

A supervisor's voice called 'forty-three pence' and Polly rang it up. The machine climaxed and spelt out a total.

'That's £15.47p, please, Mrs fforbes-Hamilton,' said Polly.

'Pence!'

Audrey got out her cheque book and began to write. Polly leant over with two rubber stamps and embossed her cheque with the name of the store and the date.

Audrey signed.

'There you are, Polly,' she said, handing the cheque over.

Polly took it and held out her other hand.

'Could I see your card?'

'My card?' She searched her bag in vain, as indeed she knew full well, since that had been withdrawn at the time of the sale.

'I appear to have left it at home,' she said. 'But surely you

175

know me,' she added with false bravura.

'Oh, I do, ma'am. I have to see the card for the number. It's the rules.'

Audrey was enraged. 'Yes, I see,' she lied. 'I quite understand.It's unfortunate that this should happen in a store that I've been coming past for years, but there it is.' She was drawing cash out of her purse. 'Oh dear, I don't seem to have quite enough money,' She looked into her trolley. 'Never mind — take out the purple sprouting.'

Brabinger handed the broccoli back and Polly docked forty-seven pence from the total.

'That's £15 exactly,' she said.

As Brabinger packed the goods into a bag, Audrey handed over the cash, which left a few pieces of loose change in her hand. Seeing the empty change scoop on its grooved arm held out in front of her, and the old instinct of patronage stirring within her, she tipped it. Then she thought better of it, and reclaimed her coins.

'No — why should I?' she moaned. 'The service was terrible.'

Back at the old lodge, the activity was akin to the quartermastering of an expedition, only in reverse. Providing rations for, say, an assault on Annapurna is a matter of deciding how long the expedition will last and then providing rations. Here was a case of somebody unpacking rations, and working out from them how long the expedition would be. It could hardly be longer than a week. Something had to happen soon.

Audrey's heart had to harden — no longer could Audrey spare Brabinger the agony of parting with the Rolls. It had to be broken to him gently. But for the moment, she was safe to set the arrangements in motion, for Brabinger was out of the way. He had excused himself saying that he had a letter to write, and she could hear him scuffing his chair in his room above the kitchen. Before long she was on the phone, dictating.

'For sale 1947 Rolls-Royce shooting Brake — good condition — one owner — no, one old lady — no, one careful chauffeur,' she was saying at writing speed. 'How on earth would I know how many miles it's done ... no, I can't ask him — offers invited. View by appointment. Marlbury 224.'

Just then Brabinger walked in. This was inconvenient — Audrey had felt confident of privacy for this call. Brabinger lived by the clock and tended to appear at the specific times allocated to his duties, or else heralded by doorbells and gongs. But now, he just materialized without preamble, in the middle of a phone call which had now to be abruptly terminated.

'Good-bye,' said Audrey curtly, and put the phone down.

Brabinger hovered. He was holding an envelope. He coughed.

'Yes, Brabinger?'

He coughed again. 'May I have a word with you, madam?'

'You appear to be having a word with me already, and while you're here, I would like to have a word with you.'

'Yes, madam?'

'Brabinger,' she said from the chair, and then stopped. She got up, dislodging Bertie from her lap, took the old man by the shoulders and steered him into the chair she had just vacated. He sat uncomfortably on the edge of the seat, clutching his envelope.

She went to the sideboard.

'Drink?'

'Certainly, madam,' said Brabinger leaping up.

'No, no, I'm getting one for you,' she hastened to say, restraining him. 'Stay where you are.'

'Not for me, madam. You know I never touch the stuff,'

177

he replied.

She poured a tot for herself and sipped it.

'Now, Brabinger,' she began. 'Dear Brabinger — I just want you to know that all the time you've worked here — well, not here, but in the manor — how long is it?'

'All my life, madam.'

'... I want you to know how much we have valued all the hard work you have done for us.'

Brabinger fidgeted in his chair, waving his envelope with the fervour of a schoolboy who knows the answer to a question but isn't being asked.

'But, madam, if...'

'Hear me out, Brabinger,' Audrey pleaded. 'After all, after so many years, it's perhaps time a thank-you was said.'

'Yes, madam. Thank you.'

'Not by you, Brabinger — by me,' It wasn't going very well, so far. 'Now, I also want you to know that I wouldn't do anything — anything in the world to upset you, or make you think I was ungrateful — you know that.'

'Yes, madam, but if I may be allowed ...'

'Wait, Brabinger. Let me say this, God knows it's hard to say, but ...'

'Madam,' interrupted the old man, 'I know exactly what you're going to say.'

'You do? How do you know?'

'It is very obvious, madam. I have known all along that things have not been exactly as they used to be.'

'How could you have known — I thought I was keeping it to myself very well.'

'It's just little things, madam — like your holiday, for instance, and the supermarket episode.'

'You are commendably perceptive — but I don't have to tell you how sorry I am it had to come to this.'

'I understand, madam. I am fully conversant with the situation and I thought it would save a lot of trouble and embarrassment if I were to make the arrangements myself.

178

Allow me, madam.'

He got up and handed her the envelope.

'What's this?' She opened it and read, then stared at Brabinger in disbelief. 'Your resignation?'

'Yes, madam.'

'You're not leaving, are you?'

'Yes, madam — I thought I'd give in my notice before I was dismissed.'

'Dismissed! But Brabinger, whatever gave you the idea I was going to dismiss you?'

'Little things, madam. For instance, being summoned here and thanked for my hard work.'

'But that's unthinkable.'

'I understood, madam, that is what you wanted to talk to me about?'

Audrey roared with laughter.

'No, no, no — oh, how absurd. Oh, Brabinger, you are priceless sometimes.'

'I try to please, madam,' he said soberly.

She fell back into an armchair laughing and Brabinger charged her glass. Bertie sprang into her lap.

'Then may I ask what it was you were going to tell me?'

Audrey sobered at once.

'Oh, it was only ...'

Her heart had so gone out to Brabinger, who was prepared to lay his livelihood on the line for her, that to tell him about the car seemed short shrift for such an act of self-sacrifice. Her eyes watered and she bit her lip.

'I forget. It can't have been very important. It's completely slipped my mind.' She shrugged her shoulders, smiled at Brabinger with almost streaming eyes and turned away.

'Oh, be off with you,' she choked.

The phone rang.

'Well, answer it, Brabinger. You're the butler round here.'

He did so.

'It is the *Marlbury and Ilcaster Messenger*, madam, about your advertisement.'

'Yes,' she said. She searched the room for inspiration and her eyes met Bertie's. 'Oh, yes, about my advertisement for a pedigree beagle. I thought Bertie should be earning stud fees — yes, thank you so much.'

Brabinger raised an eyebrow. She laughed. The corners of Brabinger's mouth began to quiver.

She grabbed the receiver.

'Oh, go and get on with your work, Brabinger.'

He did so. He went upstairs and unpacked all his suitcases again.

It wasn't until the following day that Audrey noticed what was going on over at the manor. It had rained the previous afternoon and overnight, so Maggs had to wait for the front drive to dry out a bit before he could resume filming.

They were in the kitchen washing up after lunch. This was a new experience for Audrey, and she was receiving instruction in the art, since her latest idea was that Brabinger might be able to go out to work. This would leave her with the domestic work, which she did not appear to mind.'

'Now, glasses first,' he said. 'There are no bits in the water yet, and it's hot, so that they will dry the better for it.'

'I see. I never realized there was so much theory,' said Audrey humbly.

'Oh, yes — furthermore, the tea cloth will be dry, and the glasses will not smear.'

At that moment, they saw a little, red sports car whizz past the window. Audrey instinctively kept her eyes on it and wandered into the drawing room, whence she could see the manor. As the car pulled up outside the house, it drew her attention to a great deal of activity.

Audrey put down her Friends of Marlbury Cottage Hospital tea cloth, and unearthed the binoculars from under the sofa cushions.

'Brabinger — they appear to be unloading some film cameras and lights into the manor.'

'Really, madam — I shall find out what is going on at once,' he volunteered, peering out of the window behind her.

'Would you? You'd better have an excuse.'

'I have been saving one up, madam — I could deliver Mr DeVere's invitation to the charity gala.'

'Good thinking. I'll carry on with the washing up.'

Brabinger wrenched off his rubber gloves, and took the invitation from the mantelpiece. Audrey returned to the sink. As he passed her on his way out through the kitchen door, Brabinger noticed that Audrey was about to put a decanter into the washing-up water. He leapt to rescue it.

'No, madam — if you will allow me to say so, you don't wet-wash decanters.'

'Don't you? Do you send them to the dry cleaners?'

'No, madam — you clean them with shot. Because of the narrow neck, you put pellets in and shake them around.'

'You mean lead shot?'

'Yes, madam.'

'From a cartridge?'

'Yes.'

'Cartridges as in gun?'

'Yes, madam. It's a knack.'

Audrey was baffled. 'How do you fire them in without breaking the decanter?'

DeVere came into the morning room in a Norfolk jacket and plus-fours, put down his gun, sat down in his chair and began to undo his shoelaces.

'There are some things which we British should always

be proud of,' he said earnestly to the camera. 'Our beautiful country houses for one, but there are simpler ways of preserving the traditional flavour of English life.'

He turned to the side table. It was empty.

'Where is it?' he said, stepping out of his assumed role.

'Cut,' came Maggs' rasping voice from behind the camera. 'Props! Where's the product?' He expressed his exasperation by slapping his thigh nervously, and flinging his hands in the air.

'I'm sorry, Mr DeVere. Hitchcock was right. I'm surrounded by cattle!'

Maggs thought for a moment. 'There was something missing there, don't you feel it?' he said, sucking his teeth.

'The bottle?'

'No — not the product. And you were fine, but there's something missing. Now, you remember how in "Ruggles of Red Gap" Charles Laughton played the part of ...' A thought struck him. 'Got it!' he flicked his fingers. '*That's* what was bothering me. Yes, you'll love this, everybody. What we need is ... a butler. An old English butler.'

The room filled with cries of 'Fantastic, B.M.', 'Oh, racey!' and 'Fabarooney!'

'Mr DeVere, could we use your butler?'

DeVere swallowed hard.

'Actually, I don't have ...'

There was a knock at the door. Brabinger put his head round the door and held up an envelope.

'Excuse me, Mr DeVere, Mrs fforbes-Hamilton instructs me to enquire whether you have had her invitation to the Lord Lieutenant's charity gala?'

At least, that's what Brabinger was *going* to say, but before he opened his mouth, DeVere came in with, 'Tell her I'm doing a film,' and the film crew cut him short with transports of delight.

'Perfect', 'Fantastic', 'Ruggles to the life' and 'Fabarooney'.

They were all looking at Brabinger.

'Cooee.'

Marjory was at the kitchen door of the lodge.

'Marjory, I wish you wouldn't do that,' said Audrey, looking up from *Country Life*.

'I've brought you the local paper. Thought you might like to look through the situations vacant.'

'That's not funny, Marjory.'

'You'll have to get a job soon.'

'I'll get a job the day the *Titanic* arrives, and not before.'

'And how long do you think you can hold out? Putting Bertie out to stud isn't going to make you a fortune, is it?'

Audrey raised her eyebrows. Marjory showed her the small ad under 'Pets', where the services of a beagle appeared to be being offered.

'I don't know what you're talking about, and I'll thank you not to come in here using barnyard expressions,' she snarled.

'So,' said Marjory, settling down in a very businesslike fashion, like a doctor with an uncooperative patient. 'You're looking for a job.'

'I've looked,' Audrey admitted sheepishly, revealing a folded copy of the local paper from behind her *Country Life*. 'All anybody wants are van drivers and storemen.'

'There's a receptionist and accounts person wanted here,' suggested Marjory.

'Yes — it's at the abattoir. That's a man's job, anyway.'

'Well, women are now doing jobs traditionally done by men.'

'I don't like all this sex equality — I mean, what's *wrong* with women being the dominant partners?'

'Yes, and men are doing things traditionally done by women.'

'Yes, like getting into lifeboats first,' cavilled Audrey.

'Ah, here's one,' said Marjory, running her finger down the newspaper column ' "Local architect wants a girl Friday." '

'Hopeless — one day a week's no good to me.'

Marjory's eyes strayed to another column.

'I say, do you see they're actually advertising the Lord Lieutenant's charity gala this year? By the way, will you be going?'

'No, that's for sure.'

'But isn't Mr DeVere taking you? I hear ...'

'Never mind what you hear. I have no right to expect favours from him, when I've thrown all his offers of help back in his face. He'll let me stew in my own juice now, and I can't blame him. Well,' she sighed, 'so much for ever returning to the manor. If he picked me out of this slough of despond now he'd never let me forget it. He'd use it against me. Men do. Poor Brabinger.'

'You mean poor Audrey.'

'Do I? Perhaps. The hard thing is coming to terms with it myself. It's not that I mind people laughing at me.'

'Now, now,' comforted Marjory. 'Who's laughing at you?'

'Everybody. There was that supermarket trip. Yes, you're laughing, too. When I went to the wrong restaurant on the main road the other night, why *should* I know the difference between a "Little Chef" and a "Happy Eater"?'

She looked at the charity gala advertisement.

'And now, this. It's not that I shan't be going that I mind. It's the thought that my place will be taken by some local butcher made-good who happens to own a chain of slaughter houses. Besides, there is no way I can enjoy the society of men who wear clip-on bow ties and write on lined writing paper. We have let things go too far.' She took out her handkerchief and sobbed into it.

'It's not your fault. It's just the times we live in. It's not our turn anymore. It's the price of democracy.'

'I suppose you're right.' She became defiant. 'Democracy is all very well — if only they hadn't given it to the *people*!'

At the manor, the filming session was in full swing, and Maggs was into his sixth take. Brabinger had been persuaded to participate. It had taken this many attempts to get Brabinger to make his entrance at the right point.

'There are some things which we British can always be proud of. Our beautiful country houses for one, but there are simpler ways of preserving the traditional flavour of English life.'

It was Brabinger's cue. For the first time he responded to it and shuffled forward awkwardly into vision.

'Oh, Larkin,' acted DeVere. 'Could I have my usual, please?'

'With a dash of Old English, sir?' It was the right line.

'What else?' said DeVere, holding out his glass.

'Well, some people like it with a little soda, and others ...'

'*Cut!*' shrieked Maggs. 'Give him a drink somebody — steady his nerves.'

'Gin, please,' said Brabinger, instinctively.

A production assistant rushed forward with a glass of gin, which Brabinger relished.

'Mr Larkin, you don't have to say anything there. You have one line, which you did very well, and then you just pour the drink. Now you remember Jack Buchanan in "Lord Richard in the Pantry"?'

'Who?' said Brabinger.

Maggs gave up. 'I'm surrounded by cattle,' he exclaimed to himself. 'What do these people *do* with their nights off?'

Likewise, the seventh take began well.

'... could I have my usual, please, Larkin?'

Brabinger shuffled forward and looked at the camera, divesting himself of the immortal line —

185

'Look, who *is* this chap Larkin?'

'*Cut!*' screamed Maggs. 'Once more.'

The team went through it once more, Maggs nervously awaiting Brabinger's entrance.

'... with a dash of Old English, sir?' asked Brabinger on cue with perfect timing and diction. Maggs breathed a sigh of relief as Brabinger poured the tonic water with perfection. It would have been the definitive version had not old Ned, who had been scything the grass outside the window, chosen that moment to peer in through the window with great curiosity.

But even without this intrusion, the director was not happy.

'There's still something missing in this lot,' said Maggs. The door flew open, and Mrs Polouvička flounced into the room in a long evening gown and a tiara.

'Heow kained of yoou awl to come,' she ennunciated, holding out her gloved hand to Maggs.

'I am Countess DeVere. Richard's mothaw.'

'... and that's not it,' murmured Maggs.

Audrey was getting worried. Brabinger had been gone for hours. Although it was unlikely that he had gone far because the car was still in the drive, she entertained the possibility that he might actually have forced his resignation on her by leaving. She was passing the time building a pryamid of playing cards when he came in.

'Brabinger,' she called.

Brabinger stumbled into the room, his cheeks glistening, eyes rolling and clearly the worse for a few.

'Where have you been? You only had to find out what was going on over there.'

'Yes, madam — I did find out.'

'What took you so long?'

'I found out in depth.'

'Well?'

'Mr DeVere was doing an advertisement.'

'An advertisement? What for?'

'A tonic water, madam.'

'And you've been sampling it?'

'I was invited to approve the gin, madam.'

He indicated with thumb and forefinger the measure of the amount he had taken, the gap between them widening until it took two hands to convey the impression of a quantity she was prepared to accept.

'I see,' said Audrey with some asperity.

'It's going to be very good,' Brabinger assured her with boyish enthusiasm. 'Very artistic. First there's the picture of the manor, and Mr DeVere comes in and says, 'There are several things which we British can always be proud of ...'

'Of which we can be proud,' she corrected. Then shock set in.

'We British!' she screamed in horror. 'Mr DeVere said that? He's about as English as the Brandenburg gate.'

Brabinger stood chastened.

'Do you mean, Brabinger, that Mr DeVere has dragged Grantleigh, the manor and all I hold dear, into the mire of commercialism? Really! He is quite below the salt.'

'I'm sorry, madam.'

'The shame of it. That really is the *dernier cri*. We must put a stop to this at once.'

Brabinger was abashed and he felt obliged to come clean.

'But, madam, I've just...nothing, madam.' He mumbled.

A nasty clash of views was narrowly averted, by a sound in the drive. They heard a car draw up outside. Audrey went to the window and looked out. It was a little red sports car.

'Whoever's that?'

Brabinger identified the visitor with some dread. 'It's Mr Maggs — he's the director of the commercial,'

'Who?'

'I haven't a clue, madam,'

The doorbell rang, and Brabinger did not hurry to attend to it.

'Madam, there's something you should know.'

'Answer it,' she demanded.

Brabinger went to the door by the longest route. He opened it on to himself so that he couldn't be seen behind it.

'Good afternoon, sir,' an empty space in the doorway addressed Maggs in a voice as little like Brabinger's as Brabinger could make it.

'Excuse me,' said Maggs, searching for somebody to say it to. 'My name is Maggs. I'm the director of the big film we're shooting up at the manor house. I was just passing and I ...'

A puffy hand had appeared from behind the door and beckoned him in and pointed him in the direction of the drawing room door.

'Follow me, sir,' said the voice.

'*Follow* you?'

'From, in front, sir.'

Maggs followed the direction of the finger into the drawing room.

'Mr Maggs, madam,' said the voice now hiding behind the inner door,

Audrey got up and greeted him.

'Good evening, Mr Maggs.'

'Good evening, Mrs ...'

The voice prompted him. 'fforbes-Hamilton.'

'Forgive me barging in like this,' he said handing her his visiting card, 'but I'm the director of the comm ... big feature film shooting at the manor. I'd be grateful if you could help us.'

'How?' said Audrey sternly.

'It occurred to me that all day something has been missing. In short, *we* need something *you* have.'

188

'And what would that be?'

'I was just passing and I happened to see your old Rolls.'

'Yes?'

'And I was wondering whether you would consider allowing us to use the car in the film — it would lend just the touch of class we are looking for.'

Audrey drew herself up.

'Mr Maggs, I understand that you are making a commercial?'

'Er, yes.'

'For some trifling beverage?'

'Fontleroy's Tonic — "the Little Aristocrat",' he confessed

He gave the little brush of the nose. He hoped it might be recognized but, far from giving credence, it appeared to give offence.

'Use your handkerchief. I don't know it, but even if I did, you don't think I'd allow my personal possessions to be used to disseminate lies about the dubious quality of a product.'

Maggs blushed and Brabinger's heart missed a beat.

'We'd pay, of course, we want to hire it,' Maggs assured her.

Audrey paused.

'Well, that's different.'

'Good,' said Maggs.

Brabinger's heart lifted.

'Yes, it's worse.'

'Oh,'

The interview appeared to be at an end when Audrey revived it.

'Would you like a drink, Mr Maggs?'

'Oh, thank you — whisky and soda.'

'Brabinger! Get Mr Maggs a drink, would you?'

'Yes, madam,' came the disguised voice from behind the door, which then closed.

Maggs looked in the direction of the voice, then looked at Audrey, as if seeking an explanation of her being attended by a phantom.

'The secret of a successful butler is that he should be unobtrusive,' Audrey offered.

'So you have a butler, too?' said Maggs. 'Well, well, that's two in one day. You know Mr DeVere, of course?'

'We're old friends.'

'Very obliging man. Fitted the bill exactly. Perfect English gentleman — somewhere between Oliver Reed and Wilfred Hyde-White. It's unusual to find the whole scene in one place. The English gentleman, the English manor house, the English butler.'

Audrey cringed.

'What English gentleman, what English butler?' she challenged.

'Why, Mr DeVere, and his butler ... er ... Larkin. We could have used actors but they don't have that ring of authenticity about them, do they?'

'And what, may I ask, Mr Maggs, do you know about real English butlers?'

'I was a stage hand on "The Admirable Crichton".'

'Who?'

'Kenneth More.'

'I don't know who you're talking about, but I'm sure films don't give you an inkling about how butlers go about their duties.'

'Then I can't think what does.'

'Then I suggest you watch my man, Brabinger. He is impeccable.'

The door opened and Brabinger backed in with a tray and lurked around the room, hugging the walls.

'Of course,' Audrey went on when she realized Brabinger was not disporting himself precisely as she had intimated. 'You can't expect me to approve the manor being used to line your pockets. No — it wouldn't have happened when I

190

lived there.'

'You lived there?'

'Yes — our family have owned this estate for four hundred years, until this year.'

'You mean, that Mr DeVere hasn't lived there all that long?'

'Not even one year.'

'Well, I'll be blowed,' gulped Maggs. 'We thought this was his ancestral home.'

'Gracious, no — he doesn't have one — at least not this side of Bratislava. He isn't even English. He came over here without a word of the language and lived in the East End of London. Under a tarpaulin.'

'I don't believe it.'

Brabinger was firing a soda syphon from his cover behind the armchair with spot-on inaccuracy.

'I would have thought it was obvious he came out of the wrong drawer.'

'Now you mention it, maybe. That certainly puts the mockers on the commercial a bit. I mean, what would our clients say if they found out? I could have sworn Mr DeVere was to the manner born.'

'To the manner self-taught. Almost to perfection but not quite. He still writes in green ink.'

'And what about the duchess?' he asked.

Audrey snorted.

'Mrs Polouvička — his mother, quite mad.'

Maggs sighed.

'At least, the butler was the real thing.'

'He doesn't have a butler.'

'Well, I'll be damned. Then who was the butler? He was great — a bit dithery and past it. But brilliant once he got over his nerves.'

Brabinger was pained by this description of himself.

Audrey watched as Brabinger tried to ease himself out of the door. It wasn't hard to put two and two together, when

191

one connected Maggs' conversation and Brabinger's un-characteristic furtiveness.

'Brabinger,' she shouted after him.

'Will that be all, madam?' said Brabinger hopefully and without turning round.

'No, it will not.'

Brabinger turned.

'That's the fellow,' said Maggs. 'David Niven in "My Man Godfrey" to a tee.'

Audrey appeared to be working herself up to a lambasting.

'Brabinger, have you been abusing your position of trust — not to mention degrading your profession — to sell gin?'

'No, madam. Tonic.'

Maggs intervened.

'I beg you not to be too hard on him, madam. I mean, he was well worth his money.'

Brabinger's heart sank with all hands.

'Money!' shrieked Audrey. 'Oh, I see — a bargain at thirty pieces of silver. How could you drag Grantleigh to the level of the market place for money?'

Brabinger quaked as she advanced towards him like a cobra about to spring. But her voice turned soft and sympathetic and barely audible. 'How much?' she breathed.

Brabinger took a contract from his pocket and pointed to the clause specifying the remuneration for his services.

'Glory be,' she muttered. She turned back to Maggs. 'Yes, I'm sure Brabinger was beautifully typical. I shall overlook this just once. But I don't think you should always confuse the real thing with what you see in films. I mean, our historic houses aren't occupied by dukes and duchesses any more. No, they're bursting at the seams with Arabs, Dutch, Germans, pop stars or, failing that, with businessmen recovering from nervous breakdowns or learning how to sell aircraft engines to the Chinese. So if

192

you're searching for luxurious displays of great splendour and art collections, try the Vatican and the British Rail Pension Fund.'

Maggs was backing away towards the door which Brabinger held open in a more butler-like manner.

'If it's aristocratic authenticity you want, you don't have to look further than this very room, though it's not a pretty sight.'

'I'll remember that,' said Maggs, when he was at the door.

Audrey drew back and softened her tone.

'I'm not getting at you, Mr Maggs — but it's something your principals should be told. It's just that we tire of townspeople expecting to find that we in the country are either idle rich with speech impediments or else country yokels who suck straws, wear smocks and tie their trousers in binding twine. No, it isn't the rich man in his castle and the poor man at his gate anymore; and anyway the poor man has colour television and buys dyed peas in the supermarket.'

They were in the porch. Maggs lost no time in seeking the sanctuary of his car. He got in.

'Nice talking to you,' he said, and the car drew away.

'Madam,' said Brabinger peering over the Rolls, when Maggs had gone, 'forgive my saying so — but we forgot to hire him the car.'

'I know, Brabinger,' said Audrey holding up Maggs' calling card. 'Why get a pint of milk when you can get the whole cow?'

Brabinger recognized this kind of completely un-informative lyricism. It meant Audrey had plans.

Maggs slowed up at the end of the old lodge slip road, to join the main drive to the manor. As he stopped, a voice said, 'Art 'noon sirr,' It was an exaggerated rustic burr.

He traced the sound to Ned who was scything the long grass on the bank. He was dressed in a smock, and had his trousers tied up with binding twine.

'I hear you be alookin' for country folk to be in this 'ere film o' yorn,' said Ned as he sucked his straw.

Maggs put his foot down on the accelerator, in order to put a little distance between himself and this bucolic apparition. His spurt of speed was short-lived. Suddenly he was obliged to pull up abruptly when he was about to cross paths with a procession of cows, the Home Farm herd, winding slowly o'er the Grantleigh lea.

Maggs' patience snapped. He stood up in the cab of the little sports car, clenched his fists, and beat them on the top of the windscreen, appealing to the heavens.

'I'm surrounded by cattle,' he yelled.

Ordinary life, if there ever was such a thing, at the Grantleigh estate resumed. Audrey had had good days and bad days and today, counting an even number of segments in her grapefruit and reading a cheering horoscope in the newspaper, was going to be a good day.

'I see the car workers are killing the golden goose again,' she remarked to Brabinger, who was entering the dining room with a salver of mail.

'Three browns, one window, one white with handwriting, one receipt from the garage, receipt from the GPO, one receipt from the Electricity, and I have had conciliatory overtures from Mason's Stores about the restoration of credit facilities ...'

But Audrey wasn't listening. She was reading the one-white-with-handwriting. It was from DeVere — he was apologising for having overlooked the matter, in the heat of his business commitments, but would she care to accompany him to the Lord Lieutenant's charity gala night. He had been trying to contact her by phone, but it appeared to be out of order.

'What does he mean, the phone's out of order? As if we

were the sort of people who don't pay bills,' she mumbled.

The letter was signed Hilda Green, pp Richard DeVere, and signed in his absence.

'Brabinger, I wonder if you'd like to write a letter for me,' She went to the bureau in the drawing room and took out some writing paper, and sat Brabinger in front of it with a pen.

'Dear Hilda Green,' she dictated, 'please could you inform Mr DeVere that Mrs fforbes-Hamilton would be most honoured to accompany him to the Lord Lieutenant's charity ball,'

Brabinger was writing furiously. His not to reason why.

'Now sign it.'

'Me?'

'Yes, then put pp Mrs fforbes-Hamilton and signed in her absence.'

Brabinger obliged, blotted the letter, and handed it to Audrey. She read it and laughed.

'Have I made a mistake, madam?'

'No,' she said, looking at his signature. 'It's your name. It's just that I've never really thought of you as a *Bertram*.'

'I don't *feel* like a Bertram, madam.'

Audrey stood back for a moment regarding him with great affection. Ironic that this frail old man should so symbolize everything that was good, noble, and unshakeable in the great British social structure. He was the only bastion in her life which had not fallen.

'Oh, Bertram, Bertram, Bertram.' she said. 'What are we to do?'

'Brabinger, madam, and I don't know,' replied the bastion.

Audrey wandered over to the window and looked at the manor wistfully. 'Isn't it just beautiful,' she sighed, 'I'd give anything to be back there—wouldn't it be wonderful.'

'It would, madam.'

'Well, miracles can happen and I think these ...' She held

up Brabinger's letter, '... might just be the magic words.'

'I don't follow.'

Audrey searched his face for straight answers before she came up with the question. 'Tell me, Brabinger. What do you think of our friend, Mr DeVere?'

'It isn't my place to say, madam.'

'And if it *were* your place?'

'Then I would not be a butler.'

'Don't hedge. You may speak freely. Now what do you think of Mr DeVere?'

'I do really think it is not for me to say.'

'It is if I ask you.'

'But I have no wish to distress you.'

'I see. Well, what's your honest opinion.'

'If you insist, though it's hardly for me to say and I am not given to saying hurtful things. But I believe Mr DeVere to be one of the most agreeable and discerning and gentlemenly men a butler could hope to serve. I'm sorry, madam.'

Audrey huffed and puffed. 'Thank you, but I don't think that is for you to say.'

'Cooeee!'

It came from the hall of the old lodge and wafted up the stairs. It was the night of the charity gala and Audrey was getting ready.

'I'm in the bedroom — come on up,' shouted Audrey, pouting at the dressing-table mirror to apply lipstick.

Marjory appeared in the doorway behind her. 'I wish you wouldn't do that, Marjory. It's very alarming when you live virtually on your own.'

'What.'

'You, singing out like that.'

'I wasn't singing. Surely you know when I'm singing.'

'Yes, your lips move more slowly.'

Audrey turned and inspected Marjory who was wearing a

long black dress which, where it made intermittant contact with her body, made her contours stand out like a relief map of the Andes.

'So you are going?' said Audrey.

'With the rector. I'm on my way to the vicarage.'

'I see. Is that why you're wearing a cassock?'

'Oh, Audrey, I do wish I could look like you,' she pined. 'But we are as we're made. You look lovely.'

Audrey was both flattered and guilt-ridden. 'Thank you.'

'That's a new dress isn't it?' Marjory asked.

'As a matter of fact, it is.'

'Honestly, you can't go throwing your money around like that. You can't afford it.'

'Who says I can't?'

'But the money...'

'What's money got to do with it. Don't be so coarse, Marjory. It's only people like DeVere who think about money.'

Marjory hi-hoed. It was insult-DeVere-time. She looked hard at Audrey who was busily varnishing her nails. 'I don't understand you, Audrey. Here you are, about to go out with the kindest, most considerate and well-mannered, and the best-looking man we've ever had on this estate and you're still maligning him.'

'I'd much rather go with the rector,' Audrey lied.

'Oh, what a whopper.' Marjory was getting angry. 'You know I'm right, and if you weren't such a knot of old-fashioned prejudice, you'd see it as well.'

Audrey feigned indifference to this attack and carried on with her nails. 'I don't think that was called for.'

There was a moment's pause. 'In fact,' Marjory went on bravely, 'I think you do see it. Never mind him being your only hope of getting back to the manor, I think you're secretly in love with him.'

Audrey flipped. 'How dare you,' she screamed. 'If my

nails weren't still wet, I'd throttle you for that.'

'Well, it stands to reason. For the last year you've been virtually refusing to meet the man until you can meet him on equal terms, and here you are tarting yourself up for him.'

'Your unsavoury mind is only matched by your language,' countered Audrey.

'If you ask me, you've given in. Game, set, and match to DeVere.'

'Nobody did, I haven't, and we weren't playing.'

'So what's changed?'

'Never you mind. Good Lord, is that the time?'

She was looking at the alarm clock on the bedside table and waving her left hand about to dry her nail polish. She was already ten minutes overdue at the manor.

'I must rush.' She looked at her unvarnished hand and wondered whether she should do them now or in the car on the way to the manor. Brabinger could drive. But that thought settled it. 'Better not — I don't want nail polish all up my arms.'

She did them there and then and was even later for her tryst at the manor.

To DeVere the Lord Lieutenant's charity gala was not such a socially charged event. He didn't even know what to expect. In fact he didn't give it a thought until the moment it came up in his tight schedule. In this case it was immediately after a trip abroad and his flight had been delayed. He had phoned from the airport asking his mother to do the honours if he wasn't back by the time Audrey arrived for dinner.

In the event Audrey was late, what with the nail varnish crisis, and he arrived home before she got there. He found his mother plumping up the cushions on the sofa by the fire in the drawing room, opening chocolates, and experimenting with the light dimmer to create a love-nest effect.

'How's that for timing,' he said as he burst into the drawing room having changed into evening dress — 'white tie' the invitation had said. 'Sorry I had to leave you to do everything — the plane was delayed. You don't expect fog in Saudi Arabia.'

'I've done everything I can think of,' said Mrs Polouvička proudly, and angling for praise. She took a bottle of champagne from the grate in front of the roaring fire.

'I'll open this now and let it breathe,' she said going at it with a corkscrew.

'Mother, you don't open champagne with a corkscrew.' He took it from her. It was almost boiling hot from the fire.

'Ye gods, you've boiled it!' he screamed, trying to keep the cork in and rushing out through the french window. There was a deafening report which demolished the peace of the night. DeVere reappeared with the bottle.

'That's an expensive way of keeping the sparrows off the vegetables.'

The old lady tried to look contrite.

'You don't warm champagne.'

'You're celebrating in big style, then?' said his mother, as he poured the remaining thimble-full of wine which dribbled into a glass.

'I was thinking of it. After all, it isn't every day Audrey accepts something from me, is it?'

'And see you make the most of it, son. No squabbling now.'

'That's up to her. She owes me a dusting-down. Funny, but she hasn't said a word about that commercial. Perhaps she doesn't know.'

'Of course she does — Brabinger would have told her.'

The doorbell rang. They both went to the door and opened it to reveal Audrey in a cloak and holding a cork.

'Yours, I think,' she said, returning the missile to its

owner.

'You're late,' said DeVere, resenting the advantage the cork had given her.

'It's good manners to be ten minutes late, didn't you know?'

'But you're twenty minutes late.'

'I have exceptionally good manners.'

DeVere was two-nil down, already.

The old lady bustled round.

'Let me take your coat.' she said.

Audrey disrobed revealing a magnificent garment of pink silk.

'My dear child — you look lovely,' clucked the old lady.

'Thank you, Mrs Polouvička.'

'Beautiful dress,' echoed DeVere. 'That must have set you back a few bounced cheques.'

His mother passed behind him and the pained look which shot across DeVere's face indicated that the suppression of free speech was being inflicted from the rear. Audrey looked at him guiltily.

Yes — he knew about *that*.

Mrs Polouvička suddenly felt superfluous.

'I'll be leaving you two young things alone then,' she said. 'You don't need me here playing raspberry!'

'Gooseberry, Mother.'

'Don't be cheeky.' She smiled at Audrey. 'You look a wonderful couple,' said the old lady standing back and admiring them. 'And to think, to think ...' She brushed away a tear.

'To think what, Mother?'

'There's no harm in thinking. Have a good time. I shan't wait up.' She made for the door dragging DeVere with her.

'Good night, Mrs Polouvička,' said Audrey after her.

But the old lady was whispering in her son's ear.

'Wake me up when you get in. I want to know if anything happened.' She nodded to Audrey, and said aloud, 'I'll be quite happy watching television. There's a late-night horror movie.' With that, she vanished.

'Mothers,' said DeVere, coming back towards the fireplace.

'How many have you got?' laughed Audrey.

'The one's enough.'

'Now can I get you a drink?'

'Thank you.'

'Champagne?'

'Lovely.'

DeVere took a second bottle from the cupboard.

'I say, a real Bollinger,' exclaimed Audrey.

'Surprised?'

'No, but it's amazing the number of people who get away with champagne perries these days. They taste like saddle soap.'

'You'd know, I suppose. I've never had to eat saddle soap.'

Audrey ignored the taunt.

As DeVere eased the cork out of the bottle he changed the subject.

'New dress then?'

'Yes, — nothing spectacular, but you never know it might make a line in "Jennifer's Diary" — you seem surprised.'

'I am — I thought you were one of the great *nouveau pauvre*?'

'Merely an affectation. Rich or poor, these days, it's hard to tell which is which and which one is at any one time.'

He handed her a wide-brimmed champagne glass.

'I'm sorry it's not as chilled as it might be — my mother doesn't know these things.'

'It's no matter.'

'And these are the wrong glasses. One should have tall ones to give the bubble further to go.'

'I was turning a blind eye.'

'This sort of champagne glass was designed by Louis XVI, you know.'

'I didn't.'

'They're supposed to be the exact shape and measurements of Marie Antoinette's breasts! Here's marrow in your bones.'

'And in yours,' she toasted. She drank. 'M'mm.'

'Nineteen sixty-one. A young but intelligent little champagne.'

'And old enough to vote into the bargain.' The floor was suddenly hers again. 'Of course, you know that we should be celebrating tonight. I don't suppose for a minute that you know what?'

'I do. The anniversary of the day we met.'

'Oh — you do know.'

'How could I forget?'

'Well, I thought that in order to mark the occasion, I want it understood that tonight is on me — I mean, you're providing the dinner, I think that when we get to the gala, it's only fair that should be *my* party.'

DeVere was amazed.

'What? I wouldn't hear of it.'

'Didn't you get my note?'

'I've been away. But why should you take *me*?'

'Because you've been very kind to me in the past.'

'I haven't, for God's sake — you haven't let me do anything to help you. You don't accept things.'

'Maybe, but the thought has always been there, and, as it happens, I am now in a position to reciprocate.'

'Fine — think kind thoughts and leave it at that.'

'No, I insist. Now, you were saying?'

DeVere was about to resume his overture, though not with the confidence he had before, but his preamble was interrupted by Mrs Polouvička bursting into the room waving a hot water bottle in one hand and a portable television set in the other.

202

'Look, look,' she cried.

'Yes, it's a hot water bottle,' said Audrey.

'No, no — the television — look, we're on.'

Sure enough, the picture on the screen bore out her proclamation. It was, indeed, a picture of Grantleigh Manor.

'... which have made Britain great,' the machine was saying, 'and made houses like these the symbol of that greatness. This is Grantleigh Manor.'

During some bridging music, as the camera zoomed into the manor close-up, the old lady looked at DeVere and then at Audrey.

'My boy — on television.'

The television went on. 'This is the traditional house of the fforbes-Hamilton family, and the only surviving member now lives here in the lodge.'

The picture had zoomed across the rose garden and orchard to the old lodge, then through a window into Audrey's drawing room. Audrey sat in her chair, with a side table on which stood a bottle.

'Things may not be what they were for the old British families, but there are still some things of which we British can be proud. You don't have to have a stately home to preserve the traditional flavour of English life. My usual please, Brabinger.'

An image of Brabinger appeared at her side.

'With a dash of Old English, madam?'

'What else?' said the television Audrey.

The jingle was drowned by an explosion of laughter from DeVere. Audrey was smiling smugly. Mrs Polouvička was not amused. She dug her son in the ribs, hard enough for him to stop laughing.

'I'm going to bed,' snapped the old lady stomping out of the room. 'Don't wake me up — ever!'

7

As a veteran of Lord Lieutenant's galas, Audrey did not need the many AA signs to guide her the five miles to Harborough Hall. Besides, one could see it easily from a long way off, raised as it was on its mound in the middle of its deer park and floodlighted for the occasion.

Audrey drove as usual. DeVere sat beside her, and Brabinger was in the back. She was still in her convivial mood for she was not going to miss the gala as she had thought.

'Quite like old times, eh, Brabinger?' Audrey said into the speaking tube as she approached the main gate, its wrought iron work glinting as it claimed its share of the light thrown by the flaming torches which lined the drive up to the hall. Now they were on a private road, Audrey stopped the car, and got out in order to change places with Brabinger for the final and public few yards of the approach. But as she did so, her sunny mood faded. She caught sight of something which reminded her that this was not quite like old times at all, and that, from this moment, the evening was going to take on a sinister tone.

At the side of the gates stood a sign. It said, 'Harborough Hall' but it was the next bit that she found abhorrent. In big yellow letters it said, 'For Sale, sole agents, Anderson & ffitch'. Audrey groaned.

'Oh, no — not Harborough, too. Poor Lord Mortlake — at his age. Poor Celia — at hers.'

204

Brabinger drove the one hundred yards to the hall without incident and drew up before the main steps with their massive Palladian portals. They were waved to a halt by PC Peaslake whose motorbike was parked nearby, chattering to itself.

'Good evening, constable,' said Audrey as he opened the door for her.

'Evening, Mrs fforbes-Hamilton — Mr DeVere.'

'I'm very glad we have police protection,' said Audrey.

'Could be as well, ma'am,' said Peaslake. 'Never can tell, you get safe breaking, jewel thefts, drug rackets, car thefts and all sorts under the cover of a do like this.'

'You're going to have a busy night,' said DeVere as he ushered Audrey up the flight of steps and was swallowed up by a whirlpool of music, dancing and revelling. Peaslake came round to Brabinger's side and loomed large over him to continue his inventory of crimes.

'And drunken driving isn't unheard of, either. So watch it, Mr Brabinger. Remember '47.' He directed Brabinger into the lighted paddock where other cars were parked and he found a space between a Bentley and a little mini-van with 'W. Widrig, Caterers' written on the side. As he was moving into the space, a deer scampered out of the woods behind him, and across the space into which he was edging. To avoid it, Brabinger had to swing the car over further than he intended — there was a crash, followed by a splintering of headlight glass, as he hit the little mini-van with such an impact that it rolled back several feet. Its back doors flew open hurling a wedding cake, a basin full of crockery and numerous kitchen utensils over a wide area. Brabinger leapt out to survey the damage, but PC Peaslake was on the scene almost before him.

'How many have you had, already?' asked the constable.

'Haven't touched a drop,' said Brabinger. 'I couldn't help it, only this deer jumped out on me.'

Peaslake realized that he could charge Brabinger with no

205

crime. 'I'll have you one of these days,' he warned. 'Remember '47'

'Excuse my asking,' said Brabinger innocently, 'but what *did* happen in 1947.'

Brabinger's casual tone, riled the police constable.

'No, I suppse it wouldn't have mattered a light to you. You and that car of yours.'

'What?'

'The picnic.'

'What picnic?'

' "What picnic", he says. I suppose you've forgotten that picnic for the Duke of Aldershot and Lady Dartford. Things happened.'

'They were very discreet.'

'I'm not talking about them. Other things.'

'Ah yes — Lady Bertha fell out of the car, and there was the incident of Sir Peverel and the hornet ....'

'And what were *you* doing with the car?'

'Now let me see. It was this car if I remember,' he said tapping the dented bonnet.

'So you remember that much. And what about going for a joy ride with the scullery maid.'

'Edith, yes, I remember — God rest her soul.'

'And you knew who she was.'

'Of course, she was your mother, constable. Not long married to Ned at the time if I remember.'

'Ah — we're getting somewhere. My father was in London that week-end, I believe.'

'Yes. I believe he was. And hating the traffic, if memory serves.'

'And you had the car, and went gallivanting all over the country with my mother.'

'Indeed, we returned to the manor for a corkscrew if memory serves.'

'Hah — pull the other one,' exclaimed the policeman. 'You reckoned that just because you had the car you were

Lord Muck, didn't you? You could have done what you liked with that girl.'

'It was customary, but what are you getting at?'

'It just so happens that not too many months later, I was born. I've worked the whole thing out.'

'And what are your findings?'

'I know my father never believed I was his child. It's no wonder he doesn't speak to you, and won't have you mentioned in the house.'

So all was revealed. No wonder Peaslake had a grudge against cars, particularly this one. Was it out of revenge against a man who had compromised his mother and cuckolded his father with a car that Peaslake had joined the police force, and had been persistant in his refusal to leave the Grantleigh beat? Till retribution had been meted out? No wonder he was out to rid the highways of Brabinger, and had taken so much to heart his acquittal after his last shunt. But to think that Peaslake had Brabinger down for his father.

'What's more,' the constable proceeded, 'you and my mother used to meet a lot in secret.'

'That is perfectly true,' Brabinger admitted. 'Has your father ever talked about me?'

'Your name is a dirty word in our house.'

'I thought so. Such a pity he never got over it.'

'What do you mean?'

'Things have changed so much over the years, I can hardly expect you to understand. But your father and I have been sworn enemies since I raised strong objections to your mother marrying him. It was not the proper thing for a housemaid to dally with the outdoor staff such as Ned. To be honest I thought she could have done better for herself.'

'The policeman snarled. 'You mean yourself.'

'No — that would have been out of the question.'

'Then what was it to do with you?'

Brabinger turned grave. 'You see, your mother was

207

my sister.'

Standing in a car park in the middle of the night at the scene of a minor traffic accident and knee-deep in bits of broken glass, wedding cake, and kitchen utensils, is not the ideal setting for the shattering of a myth on which one had built one's entire life.

Peaslake felt ridiculous. So much for his prospects with the CID. He'd done his detective work, but got it all wrong. He fell silent and stared at Brabinger in disbelief. Far from being humbled and apologetic, and calling off the vendetta forthwith, he intensified it. It now became a family feud, in which he took his father's part. This humiliation was worse than the alleged offence itself. Peaslake seethed more virulently than before, and instantly became even more determined to get even with the old butler.

'Forget '47,' he warned with the same malevolence with which he normally urged him to remember it.

Unable to charge him with careless driving, for this was a private estate, Peaslake looked round him for some other offence to pin on his apprehendee. Wilful damage occurred to him, but casting his eye over the debris lying on the ground between the two vehicles he saw something which changed his mind. Lying on the grass in the darkness he could see a piping syringe, a utensil such as the Widrig people might use for icing cakes. It was a foot long and the cylinder of orange plastic was a good two inches wide. It had a decorative star nozzle.

'What's this then?' accused the constable, holding the syringe aloft. 'You're not on drugs are you, Mr Brabinger?'

The difference between the charity gala night and any other social function in the neighbourhood is simply a matter of scale. Everything from the guests themselves to those who attended to their needs, from the band to the caterers were exactly the same. On one side were the Arnolds, Andersons and rectors of this world — and on the other were the Widrigs and the Cartwrights and Peaslakes. The only changing feature of any of these gatherings was the venue, and tonight it rose in importance since Harborough was the most luxurious house in the neighbourhood. Some, notably Audrey, would say that it lacked the one great luxury of homeliness which in their view made somewhere like Grantleigh preferable. The human being is a difficult creature to satisfy. But those who were given to admiring their surroundings, their presence at Harborough presented an opportunity to strike a richer seam of conversation. For the rest, there was nothing to distinguish the substance of their chatter from that at any other party.

'Does your horse go to school?' shrilled a voice.

'And Gerald said, quick as a flash, oh duvet?' came another.

'Now, there are the Fairweathers, but I don't see the Pocklingtons. Perhaps they're at the Wymms-Wellbourne wedding.'

But since her encounter with the 'For Sale' sign, Audrey was not disposed to indulge in banal chatter. She was incensed by the meaningless prattle going on around her in the face of the ultimate fate. As she danced a waltz with DeVere, her mind was on other things, and she remained silent.

'A guinea for your thoughts?' said DeVere sweeping her lifeless body through a spin turn. Audrey came out of her reverie and questioned the price.

'Inflation,' he explained.

'Actually, I was thinking of the Serpentine in Hyde Park on a hot day.'

'What made you think of that?'

'I've quite often seen pictures in books of the good old British people asleep in deck chairs, and they always seem to be taken the day before war is declared. Have you noticed that?'

'Can't say I have. What about them?'

'Asleep, eyes closed. Newspapers on their faces, not to mention wearing braces in public. Or if they're awake, it's all eating and drinking and being merry, for tomorrow we die.'

'You're being morbid.'

'Yes, and rightly. Those people with knotted hand-kerchiefs over their eyes are like this lot.'

A loud voice boomed in the distance. 'Damn good shoot, this. Barrels get bloody hot.'

'And the hunt — dashed good three days a week country.'

It was a remark which Audrey claimed as evidence of her point.

'They don't seem to know what's happening — or care. This time next year, this building will probably be pulled down, and its treasures will be spread all over the globe,' she pointed to the ceiling. 'How do you think that Crystal de Roche chandelier would look like in a Bedouin tent?'

'I see,' said DeVere solemnly.

'Honestly, Richard, it does make my blood boil. This place will go the way of all the rest and before we know where we are it will be in the hands of some foreigner.'

DeVere threw her a questioning glance.

'Oh, I'm sorry, Richard,' she apologised, detaching herself from him and bringing their dance to a standstill. She stood amazed. 'I was forgetting, I had honestly completely forgotten.' Suddenly, all thoughts of his being a foreigner had vanished. Brabinger and Marjory had been right. It was easy.

From that moment, he seemed to be within the pale. What's more, he hadn't once trodden on her toes while they were dancing, though she had been too abstracted to realize it at the time.

'You dance very well,' she complimented him.

'Then why are we standing here, talking?' He was about

210

to lead her back on to the dance floor, when they caught sight of the Lord Lieutenant and Lady Mortlake bearing down on them.

'Oh, do let me introduce you to some friends,' said Audrey.

'Hello, Audrey. Lovely to see you,' gushed the radiant Lady Mortlake.

'Hello, Celia, dear,' said Audrey as the two women joined cheeks and kissed the air beside the other's ear. 'Celia, I'd like you to meet ...'

'Hello, Richard,' the hostess whinneyed.

'Oh, you've met.'

'We're old friends,' agreed Lord Mortlake. 'Good to see you, Richard,' he said, shaking his hand vigorously.

The old man turned to Audrey and held out his hand.

'And you are ...?'

Audrey clenched her teeth which transformed her smile into a mechanical, almost metallic, sham. Her smile played about her lips but faded from her eyes. It was for Lady Mortlake to save the situation.

'Audrey fforbes-Hamilton. You remember, darling, from Grantleigh Manor ... as was.' The reminder of Grantleigh 'as was' did nothing to revive her spirits.

'Yes, of course, of course,' spluttered the old man. 'Memory isn't what it was, you know. But maybe that's an advantage sometimes.'

'Yes, isn't it sad,' she said.

'What?' asked Lady Mortlake.

'That the hall is up for sale?' The old man offered his explanation without remorse.

'Had to happen in the end. Not so bad for me, of course. I'll be dead and gone soon, but it's not going to be pleasant for Celia. I mean having to leave while you're still young enough to manage the stairs — what?'

He laughed, but they could see that having to leave the hall would require bigger adjustment on his part than dying. He was already looking about him as if taking a last look at the remaining vestiges of his family history.

'Might as well quit while you're ahead,' he went on. 'Still no use crying over spilt money. Let's enjoy ourselves while we can. How about a dance, Audrey?' Audrey looked at her partner for consent. DeVere nodded and the Lord Lieutenant ushered her on to the dance floor. DeVere was left with Lady Mortlake.

'Would you like to dance?' asked DeVere.

'Would you mind frightfully if we didn't?' said Lady Mortlake, thrusting her large bosom at him. 'Let's sit this one out. I'd like to talk to you.'

The band which had been instructed to keep things traditional, was playing 'Mountain Greenery' — a quick-step.

Audrey and the Lord Lieutenant swirled with the best of them within the ability of a seventy-eight-year-old. She felt a curious affinity with him. The knowledge that he would soon be going through the same kind of trauma as she'd now come to terms with made her feel like the elder statesman. She also thought that her counsel would be very much in demand by Lady Mortlake on the old man's demise. And, of course, there was always the chance that he would die tomorrow, in which case she would have to leave the hall, unless of course she was lucky enough to remarry somebody who could afford to buy it and thereafter to run it. Audrey looked over at the table where Lady Mortlake had been sitting with DeVere. There were two empty chairs. With each twist and turn of their quickstep, Audrey scanned the room in search of them.

She saw them at the top of the great staircase walking along the gallery with Celia Mortlake on DeVere's arm. DeVere appeared to be inspecting the premises, pointing and gesturing and showing interest in the architecture and the pictures and furniture for all the world as if he was thinking of buying the place.

'Oh, my God,' gasped Audrey. The blood drained from her as she sensed she may have stumbled on the truth.

'*Was* he thinking of buying the place?'

'What, what, what,' said the old man, as Audrey went white, felt weak at the knees and sagged in his arms.

'Are you all right?'

'Excuse me Lord Mortlake, it's the heat. I'll be all right.'

'Well, as I was saying ...'

Audrey wasn't aware that he'd been saying anything. She was only aware of a horrific realization that DeVere could be about to do the same here as he had already done at Grantleigh.

'He can't be, he can't be,' she kept repeating, prayerfully and with anguish.

But the evidence which rushed to her mind only confirmed her worst fears. Hadn't Celia Mortlake said they were 'old friends'? Hadn't she been aware that there was another woman in his life? And wasn't it only a matter of a few years before DeVere would be able to have both the desirable Lady Celia Mortlake *and* Harborough Hall? And by comparison, surely Audrey fforbes-Hamilton and Grantleigh Manor were pretty small beer.

Audrey began to kick herself for being so over-confident of her own desirability. She had been playing DeVere along for too long and now it looked as if she was being out-manoeuvred. Losing face by being the first to weaken now mattered not a jot. There was no time to lose. Abstracted by these thoughts, she had not been giving a full measure of concentration to the dancing, which she was now doing with such ferocity that she had taken the lead from the seventy-eight-year-old. She had been spinning him round the dance floor in a frenzy and the old man was groping for balance, gasping for breath.

It was a chastening moment when she realized that she was man-handling to an early grave the very man whose continued health and long life were so essential to her own ambitions. She slackened the pace, with such velocity that this, too, almost had the effect she most feared and from this moment of truth to the end of the dance seemed like an eternity.

When that welcome moment arrived, the Lord Lieutenant escorted her back to the table, meeting DeVere and Lady Mortlake at the bottom of the stairs en route.

'Thank you, Lord Mortlake,' said Audrey graciously, and without a hint of urgency.

'My pleasure,' said the old man, still fighting to recover his breath.

'Please don't let Richard and I detain you. I am sure you have other guests you wish to speak to,' Audrey went on with particular reference to Lady Mortlake who was still clutching DeVere's arm.

'On the contrary,' said Celia Mortlake, 'we have been having a most interesting conversation.'

'Is that so?' returned Audrey acidly, as the band struck up 'Tea for Two'. 'I think they said this was to be a gentleman's excuse-me.'

With that, DeVere found himself being dragged away on the dance floor. He and Audrey linked arms and disappeared into the formless mass of bodies bumping into each other like cells in a bloodstream. They danced rapidly a quarter of the way round the floor before DeVere was frog-marched through a french window on to the balcony.

'Audrey, what are you doing? You're hurting me.'

'I'm sorry, but this is very important,' said Audrey.

She let go of his arm which he rubbed to restore the circulation halted by her vicelike tourniquet of fingers.

He took in his new surroundings.

'I get the impression you want to tell me something?'

'Oh, so much, so much, I don't know where to begin.'

Audrey took hold of herself and smiled at him as if to expunge all record of the violence by which their presence on the traditionally romantic balcony scene had been

214

affected. She took a deep breath.

'We've known each other a long time, Richard.'

'A year.'

'Long enough,' said Audrey.

'In a lifetime, a mere bagatelle.'

'But during that time we have both been through a lot, and got to know each other.'

'Yes.'

'And during that time, Richard, I'm afraid to say, that I've treated you shabbily, but shabbily.'

'So?'

'I want to apologise.'

'Whatever for?'

'For being me.'

'What brought this on?'

'Never mind that. I just want to say I'm sorry. I have done some very cruel things to you and said some unkind things which were totally unjustified. Huh. As if you were the sort of man who *would* mend his motorbike in the drawing room. Anyway I'm sorry. I've been thoroughly headstrong, difficult, petulant and bitchy.'

'But ...'

'Yes, I said it. Bitchy. There's no other word.'

'I don't understand,' said DeVere.

'... And meanwhile, you've been patient, and understanding and the perfect gentleman, and,' she choked, '... oh, how can I ask you to forgive me?'

'Look, Audrey — I don't know what's got into you, but I hate to see you like this.'

'No, no — I don't deserve your pity,' she went on. 'Let me say I'm sorry — I have been very hard on you.'

'And has it occurred to you that that's what I like about you?'

'What do you mean, "like" — you have no right to 'like' me.'

'Well, I do — I'm sorry. And do you know why? Because

215

you're about the only woman I've ever known who's given me a good fight.'

She rounded on him with curiosity.

'What do you mean?'

'What I like about you. Because you're tough. Because what you've been through in the last year would have broken weaker people. You've refused to let that happen. You won't be browbeaten, or defeated. You've gone from one extreme to the other, and you haven't shown any signs of it. No one would know — except me, of course.'

'Oh, how come you noticed?'

'It takes one to know one. We're two of a kind — we're winners. We're survivors. I've always said that if you and I could get together, we could make a good team.'

'How was I to know that — you haven't told me?'

DeVere's eyes rolled, he spun a full circle on his heels, with his arms stretched towards the moon.

'Give me strength,' he prayed. He turned back to Audrey. 'Isn't this where I came in?' he breathed. 'What do you think I've been trying to do for the last year?'

Audry gulped.

'I had no idea.'

'Then it's time you did.'

'You mean, you don't hate me?'

'Quite the opposite. But since we're laying all our best cards, I'll tell you something else. You and I have something else in common. You lost a husband — I lost a wife — and we've both had to deal with that this year.'

'Is that relevant?'

'Of course, it is — you fool,' He looked her full in the face. 'But I think one should allow the paint to dry before putting on a second coat. Do we understand each other?'

'Oh — we do — we do. Wonderfully,' she proclaimed.

He took her hand and steered her towards the window.

'Now, how about another dance?'

She stopped and detached herself from him.

216

'No — not yet. There's something else I want to tell you. I have been harbouring very unjust thoughts about you.'

'So? What's new?'

'No — hear me out.'

'We'll be here all night.'

'How lovely.' DeVere leant against the ivy-clad wall with his arms folded as for a long consultation. Audrey spoke on with great earnestness.

'In my heart, I have accused you of carrying on, shall we say, with Celia Mortlake.'

DeVere snorted.

'And worse. I was wrong, I know, but I thought that you were crafty enough and snob enough to be capable of cultivating her so that when, in the near future, the Lord Lieutenant ...' she faltered.

'Passes on?'

'If you like — then you would marry Celia, having bought Harborough Hall in the same villainous way ... sorry ... the same perfectly legal way you bought Grantleigh.' She paused. 'I take it all back — I'm sorry. Celia Mortlake — huh!' she chuckled dismissively.

DeVere was smiling. He laughed.

'Funny, isn't it?'

'Yes.'

'That's a very good idea — it's the best thing you've said all night.'

Audrey's smile faded.

'What do you mean?'

'Well, I hadn't thought of that. I mean, who needs Grantleigh? Celia Mortlake, eh!'

He looked in at the dance hall and saw her lugging the old Lord Lieutenant round the floor.

'You're not serious?'

'Of course I am,' he said, playfully. 'I'm a villain — remember?'

Audrey was suddenly in no mood to be toyed with.

217

'Just a minute,' she pleaded. 'What's she got that I haven't got?'

'Much the same. A big house, youth, beauty, style, breeding, class, good connections ....'

'Oh, I see,' screamed Audrey, her anger suddenly boiling over. 'So that's all you're after, is it? It's just as well we discussed it in time, eh? You don't think I'm going to make myself a step in your social climb, do you? You foreign upstart — so what do you think you've got which makes you so attractive to me?'

'Money and Grantleigh Manor — but not necessarily in that order, but nonetheless useful to the British downstart.'

'I see, so this was just going to be a little business arrangement, was it?'

'Now, steady, Audrey.' He held her in the doorway. Her eyes blazed.

'Let go of me, you rake, or I'll scream.'

'You are screaming.' He let go.

'Go to Lady Mortlake if you must. Just leave me out of your plans. And don't bother to come after me.'

With that, she slipped through the french window and was gone.

'Look — can't you take a joke?' DeVere asked rhetorically after her.

She looked lovely when she was angry, he thought.

In the dance hall, Audrey, bursting with rage, fought her way through a hideously banal Gay Gordons, making a bee-line for the door. Finding a gap between dancers, she made for it, only to be mowed down by the ebb and flow of circulating couples, way-haying inanely. She reclaimed her coat, ran down the main steps of the portico, passed Peaslake's chattering motorcycle and across the lawn into the car park. Audrey got in the car and slammed the door.

Brabinger peered at her through the windscreen from the

front of the bonnet, where he appeared to have been crouching.

'Home, Brabinger,' she barked. 'Get me away from here. Get me away from that man.'

'But, madam, we have no headlights. I'm afraid we've broken them,' he whimpered, showing the broken bulbs and shards of glass.

'Never mind — let's make tracks.'

'The road, madam?' enquired Brabinger.

'Yes, Brabinger — the road.'

'You mean, the Queen's highway, madam?'

'Yes, yes,' she screamed.

'A public thoroughfare, madam? With other traffic on it? Cars and that sort of thing?'

'Yes, Brabinger, for heaven's sake. All the way home. Now, get moving.'

Brabinger got in, started the car and moved out of the car park past the hall, giving a wide berth to the Peaslake motorcycle, then proceeded down to the lodge and through the wrought iron gates by the 'For Sale' sign.

Then, joy of joys, it was the open road.

Brabinger steered the car nervously on to the forbidden main road, and proceeded on one dim headlight. Audrey was still looking out of the back window and could still see Harborough Hall behind them, perched on its mound in the deer park and bathed in floodlight, from a long way off.

'Let DeVere have it,' she was muttering to herself. 'Let him have her,' she thought. 'There will be other fishes in the sea for Grantleigh, and what's more, they might have more meat on them.' Then, 'Faster, faster, Brabinger. Get me away from here.'

Brabinger was on the crest of euphoria as he felt his foot on the accelerator and savoured the sensation of speed and the power of the Rolls engine in front of him — fifty...sixty ...seventy...eighty...ninety miles an hour. His moment of ecstasy was short-lived, for now behind them they could hear the wail of a police siren.

Brabinger slowed the car down to fifty and the police motorcycle overtook them. In his one dim headbeam he could see he was being waved down. Brabinger pulled up behind it and switched the lights off, in the faint hope that the defect would not be noticed. There was silence and darkness. Just his luck: to be caught on this one occasion when Audrey wasn't in the driving seat. He did not dare look up as he heard the tread of authority coming back towards him — but he suddenly realized that the dark figure was not coming to the driver's side. Already the passenger door was opening and somebody was sitting down beside him. Oh, why hadn't Audrey been driving! In the darkness it was only the voice which told him who the figure was.

'I'll say this for you, you're lovely when you're angry!' said Richard DeVere, and tapped Brabinger on the knee.